Joan O'Neill

BREAD & SUGAR

**Hodder
Children's
Books**

a division of Hodder Headline Limited

Come away, O human child!
To the waters and the wild
With a faery, hand in hand,
For the world's more full of weeping than you
*   can understand.*

William Butler Yeats, 'The Stolen Child'

Acknowledgements

For their help, support and encouragement, my sincere
thanks go to: my family and the O'Neill family; my
agent, Jonathan Williams; my editor, Nicole Jussek; Philip
MacDermott and all the staff at Poolbeg Press; my writers'
group: Maureen Keenan, Mary Kirby, Jackie Dempsey,
Rita Stafford, Ann Cooper, Sheila Barrett, Alison Dye,
Phil McCarthy, Cecilia McGovern; Katie Donovan,
Cathy Leonard and the Bray Literature Group; the
International Red Cross (Central Tracing Agency);
the staff of Deansgrange Library; the Security Guards
at the Royal Naval Hospital, Gosport; Clare Donelan,
for her information on nursing TB patients in Newcastle
Sanatorium during Dr Noel Browne's term of office; Al
Morris of Bray Cabs, for his information on boxing; my
sister-in-law, Winnie Kelly, for her unflagging support; all
my friends, with particular mention to Barbara and Kim,
Norma, Rose, Sandra, Patty, Shane and Tanith. A special
thanks to Mary Rose Callaghan and Liz McManus.

For my children, Gerard, Jonathan,
Robert, Elizabeth and Laura,
with my love and gratitude

1

The taxi was late. It was an early morning in February 1948 and the sun shone in a cloudless sky, promising warmth. Tufts of smoke rose from chimneys along the terrace, quiet because the children were at school.

'Is there no sign of it, Lizzie?' Mam's voice was quick with impatience as she called out to her daughter.

'No. Not yet.' Lizzie shut the door on the draught.

'They should be here by now. I hope to God nothing's happened to them.'

Mam came into the hall, looking elegant in her new frock. 'Do I look all right? This perm is very frizzy. Oh, I wonder what John looks like now.' She gazed at her reflection in the hallstand mirror. 'There's a lot of grey in my hair.'

'You're grand, Gertie.' Dad came downstairs, and looked into the mirror with her.

'Go on with you. I've aged ten years since they went to the States. I can see it myself.'

'Not as far as I'm concerned you haven't.'

1

'You always were a bit of a flatterer, Bill Doyle.' She smiled with pleasure.

The sound of a car coming down the street sent her rushing to the door, and down the steps. Just as she reached the gate, the car slowed down, the gears protesting as it came to a halt. 'Is this number 30?' The driver leaned out of the window, and squinted at her through the smoke of the cigarette that was glued to his lips.

Mam moved forward. 'Of course it's the right house.' Her voice was excited and expectant all at once.

The taxi door opened and Karen alighted, pulling her silver fox fur coat around her. Behind her John, her nine-year-old son, tumbled out and almost pushed her aside as he rushed into Gertie's arms. 'Gertie, Gertie, I'm home!'

'Oh, my little darling, it's wonderful to see you!' Gertie leaned forward to enfold him in her arms. Straightening herself, she said, 'Let me look at you. You've grown so tall. Bill, hasn't he grown? And the colour of you!'

John, tall for his age, beamed as they inspected him.

'He's marvellous.' Bill Doyle lifted him up in the air.

'Hey, watch out for your back! I'm heavier now.'

'You certainly are. Did you like North Carolina?'

'It was OK I guess.'

'You've picked up quite an accent. A real little Yank.' Bill lowered him and turned to Karen. 'How's my girl?' They embraced.

'It's so good to see you, Dad, and you too, Mam.' Karen went to hug her mother, leaving the tall man by her side standing alone.

'You must be Hank.' Bill extended his hand.

Mam said, 'You're very welcome,' as she in turn shook his hand.

'Thank you, Ma'am,' Hank drawled. 'It sure is a pleasure to meet you all at last.'

'It's great to be home.' Karen discreetly wiped a tear from her eye.

The taxi driver opened the boot and began lifting out the luggage. Lizzie, Karen's younger sister, not wanting to intrude on the moment her parents had been waiting for, came out of the house and almost collided with the taxi driver. 'I'll help with the luggage,' she offered.

'I can manage, love,' he said, heaving and hauling the cases up the steps, his spindly legs zig-zagging under the weight, his cigarette stuck to his lips.

'Lizzie!' Karen ran to her. 'It's great to see you! I want you to meet Hank.' She linked his arm, pushing him forward at the same time. Hank smiled, flashing gleaming white teeth. 'I've heard so much about you, Lizzie.'

There was something familiar about his handsome features. Suddenly it occurred to Lizzie that, apart from his colouring, he resembled Paul, especially around the eyes.

'Let's go inside,' Gertie said. 'It's chilly.'

Dad and John mounted the steps, John chattering all the time about the enormous ship and the endless sea they had travelled across.

As Mam prepared the breakfast, Lizzie set the table. Karen stood before the quietly simmering Aga, warm and welcoming to her outstretched hands, and took in every detail of the kitchen. Suddenly she said, 'Where's Gran?'

'In her room.'

Karen made for the stairs.

'Karen.' Mam's voice detained her. 'She's fast asleep. She sleeps so badly nowadays that we don't bother to call her.'

'That's sensible. I'm dying to see her though.' She sat down and allowed herself to be distracted by John, whose delight at being home manifested itself in racing about, opening doors, inspecting everything.

'The house is alive again.' Mam eyed him indulgently, a catch in her voice. 'Stand still a minute, John, and let me have a good look at you.'

He stood there, hair neatly combed, blue eyes luminous with mischief.

'You're back!' Gran hobbled into the kitchen and stood there, clutching her walking stick, her eyes a feast of looking.

Gran was Bill's mother. She was eighty-five years old, alert, but sometimes unpredictable. She talked to herself a

4

lot. When she reminisced about 'the old times' and her scattered family, she became sentimental. At other times, when she'd had a tot of whiskey, she would rage about the Troubles, the war, and Karen's husband, Paul, who had gone missing in action, nine years before in France. 'I'll never believe he's dead, until I see it confirmed on paper,' she said. 'He was far too lively.'

'The war has no consideration for age, or beauty,' Dad told her, but she would not listen.

'Is there any word of Paul?' she would say and Mam would always reply 'No' with a heavy sigh, and to Lizzie, 'It's just as well Karen doesn't have to listen to her.'

'Gran's becoming a burden on Mam. She's getting worse,' Lizzie confided to Dad.

She was. She wandered around the bedrooms at night, pulling at the blankets on their beds when they were asleep, urging one or other of them to get up and get dressed. 'Hurry, Lizzie,' she would say. 'Your uncle Tommy's at the front door.' Or, 'Your grandad's back at last. Let him in before he catches a chill.'

Sometimes she spent hours gazing up the road, holding the curtains with a frail hand, as if she was expecting someone.

'I can't put her in a home. I'd be too ashamed,' Mam protested when Dad suggested discreetly that she needed proper nursing care. 'Anyway, we'd miss her terribly, and she'd fade away and die without us.'

She had waited for Karen and John's homecoming with the same growing impatience as the rest of the family. When their return had been postponed, the family had accepted it. But when Karen wrote repeatedly with various reasons why they would not be coming back yet, Mam got very annoyed. Even Dad, who always found an excuse for Karen's behaviour, began to lose patience. 'It's a long time since she sent that first telegram to say they were coming home to get married.'

'Hank seems to be heavily involved in the timber business,' Mam said. 'At least he takes his work seriously.'

'I hope he takes our daughter seriously and brings her home where she belongs. We don't even know if his intentions are honourable.'

'I'm sure he won't hurt her,' Gran said. 'She's been through so much already. Hank realises that. After all, he's Paul's cousin, Gertie. She's not dealing with a stranger.'

'You've mellowed, Gran. Do you remember when Karen first met Paul? You weren't too keen on him,' Gertie reminded her.

'I hadn't met him and the circumstances were different.' Gran looked uneasy. 'What happened then will never happen again. She's learned some hard lessons, poor child.'

Now Gran slowly came into the room, held out her arms and Karen went to her, holding her in a gentle embrace. John stood, good as gold, waiting to be hugged.

'I'm afraid that if I close me eyes, you might disappear on me. I prayed for you all the time you were away.' Gran's sharp eyes looked at each of them in turn.

'I know you did, Gran.' Karen gave her a loving look.

'Thank God I lived to see Paul returned to us.' Her eyes clouded over as she gazed at Hank.

'This is Hank, Gran. Paul's cousin,' Karen said, in a wistful voice.

'Of course it is.' Gran beamed and held out her hand. 'You're welcome home,' she said as he stood up to greet her. She straightened herself, with obvious effort.

'Come and sit down.' Hank pointed to the chair beside him.

Gran seated herself, her bones creaking painfully, and leaned toward Hank. 'You're so like Paul.' She smiled at him.

'So they tell me.' Hank smiled back.

'What do you think of Karen's home? Paul loved it, for the short time he was here, poor boy.'

'Give the man a chance!' Mam began serving rashers, sausages and eggs from a huge plate. 'He's only in the door. Come and sit down everyone, and have your breakfast. You sit here, Hank, and when you've eaten, I'll show you to your room. I've put you in the room at the top of the house. It's very comfortable up there.'

'And quiet. You won't be disturbed by that little tiger.' Dad winked at John.

'You're in your own room, Karen, with John,' Mam continued. 'Of course, after you're married, you can have the double room on the return. We had it redecorated.'

'They slept in the same bedroom in North Carolina,' John informed everyone, as he tucked into his rashers and eggs. 'They even slept in the same bed.'

'Am I hearin' things?' Gran cried.

'How many times have I told you not to speak out of turn?' Hank snarled at John, his mouth a nasty twist of anger.

Karen blushed. Hank stared at his plate.

Mam opened her mouth, then shut it again, swallowing her irritation. She said, 'I see,' knowing that to lose her temper would cause a flood of arguments.

'Well, soon you'll be married,' Dad said.

Hank cleared his throat. 'Not immediately, sir. I have some business to attend to here and in Norway, so we thought we'd get that out of the way first.'

'What?' Mam went pale.

'What sort of business?' Dad's voice was sharp.

Hank's eyes met his. 'I'm a tree farmer, sir. I'm interested in planting trees, land reclamation, forestry and drainage. I'm thinking of buying some land here and in Norway.'

'Isn't your farm in America big enough?' Gran asked.

'It sure is,' John cut in, spreading his hands wide, almost knocking Gran's cup from her hand.

'John, don't interrupt.' Karen was cross.

8

Hank continued talking, addressing himself to Bill. 'I want to buy some land here and plant spruce, pine and larch. They're fast-growing trees for cropping, and very suited to the Irish climate and soil. Forests planted on barren or reclaimed land, with proper drainage systems, would enrich the soil, give employment.'

Gran looked perplexed. 'Why plant trees here when you live in America?'

Hank put down his knife and fork and, looking from one to another, patiently explained. 'There's a demand for timber in the construction industry, with all the rebuilding there's been since the war. Transmission and power lines are carried on forestry poles. Land here is cheap. I might buy land already planted, if I can get what I'm looking for. Now is the time to buy. Then I could export to Europe.' He spoke animatedly, igniting Bill with his enthusiasm. Taking a map of Ireland from his pocket, he showed Bill the planting areas shaded in various colours.

Bill was impressed. 'You've put a lot of thought and work into this project, Hank. Do you have the right contacts?'

'I've been in touch with the Forestry Division of the Department of Lands.'

'Foreigners buyin' up our land. I'm not sure if Mr de Valera would sanction that,' Gran announced. 'He said the nation should depend on itself. He knows what he's talkin' about. Grand man, Mr de Valera.'

Bill frowned. 'We have an inter-party government now. Mr MacBride is hoping to secure post-war American financial assistance, with his plans for the expansion of forestry. I think you have a good idea there, Hank. The Irish farmers aren't interested in forestry in my opinion. They just want to farm their parcels of land and be left alone.'

'They're a lazy lot,' said Gertie. 'Always complaining.'

'They have it hard, Gertie. Out in all weathers, working night and day. What do they know about forestry anyway?'

'They'll have to be told then, won't they?'

'Sure,' Hank said. 'A retraining programme is being formulated.' He took a wallet full of addresses from his jacket's inside pocket. 'I have to see George Garnett, the American Minister to Ireland, and the Irish Minister for Forestry.'

'When are you planning on going to Norway?' Mam asked.

'Possibly next week.'

'Next week!'

'It'll be great to have Karen and John to ourselves again.' Gran beamed at the uncomfortable Hank.

'I'm going with Hank.' Karen looked defiantly at Mam.

'So you've made your plans?' Mam addressed Karen.

'Yes.'

'Are you taking John?'

'I thought—' Karen stopped and looked helplessly at Dad.

'You might as well go. We'll take care of John. It'll give you a break on your own.' Dad squeezed her hand.

'Thanks, sir,' Hank said. 'Much obliged.'

John looked startled. 'How long will you be gone?'

'As long as it takes Hank to find something suitable, darling.' Karen gave him a hug.

'Sounds like a good idea to me.' Dad looked at Mam in a placatory way.

'Then there is nothing more to be said.' Gertie sucked in her breath and stood up. 'I'd better light the geyser. I'm sure you'd like a bath, Karen, after your long journey.' She marched out of the kitchen.

Karen shivered. 'Oh dear, I'm afraid I've upset her.'

'That's nothing new.' Gran sniffed. 'She was lookin' forward to the weddin'. A celebration like that is important to the whole family, Karen. She had everythin' planned.'

'It's only postponed,' Karen protested. 'We didn't cancel it.'

'Why can't I come with you, Mom?' John blinked back the tears that were forming in his eyes.

'You have to go to school, darling. We'll be back before you know it.'

'She still had to let people know it was postponed,' Gran continued relentlessly. 'Of course, that didn't suit them at all. There was talk.'

'That's enough, Mother.' Bill shot her a disapproving look, but Gran said, 'I speak as I find'.

Karen was so irritated by Gran's remonstrance that she left the kitchen, making some excuse about unpacking. She beckoned to Hank to follow her. He closed the door behind them, but not before telling John to behave himself while they were out of the room. John grimaced and, as soon as they were out of earshot, said, 'I hate him'.

Bill looked appalled. 'That's a terrible thing to say. You can't mean it.'

'Yes I do. Mom says I must do what Uncle Hank tells me, but it sure is hard to remember everything. He's ratty.'

'Is he now?' Gran studied John's earnest face. 'In what way?'

'He says children should be seen and not heard. That sort of stuff. And the other day he hit me for no reason. Honest, Gran.'

'He what?'

'I'm sure you're exaggerating, John,' Dad said. 'Hank wouldn't hurt you.'

John lowered his head, his bottom lip protruding. 'He won't let me suck my thumb.'

'Well,' Bill laughed, 'you're getting a bit old for thumb sucking.'

'Never mind,' Gran said. 'Patsy'll be here soon. That'll be company for you.'

John looked up. 'Who's Patsy?'

Gran was distracted by the footsteps up and down the stairs, doors opening and closing, bits of inaudible conversation between Hank and Karen, or Karen and Mam.

'Isn't it wonderful to hear the sounds of livin' in this old house again?' Her eyes shone with happiness. 'There's nothin' like children to liven up a place. I remember when Vicky came over during the Emergency as if it was yesterday.'

'Who is Patsy, Gran?' John was getting impatient.

'A family your parents know, the Quinns, were having a hard time of it, so Gertie offered to help them out. Gertie and Mrs Quinn are in the Legion of Mary together. Patsy's one of their children.' Gran had an infuriating habit of assuming that everyone else was privy to all the family information.

Someone clumped downstairs and Gran said, 'Sssh, don't say anything. Gertie hasn't told Karen yet.'

Lizzie came into the room. 'I'm going down the town. Are you coming, John?'

John leaped from the table. 'I'll get my coat.'

Bill and Gertie had spared no expense when they were redecorating the house, painting the outside, wallpapering, having the sofa in the sitting-room re-upholstered. All for Karen's wedding. Although they never complained, the upkeep of the house was becoming a financial burden. There were always problems with the roof: as soon as one leak was repaired, there was another one somewhere else and the gutters needed replacing. Getting a tradesman was very difficult. So many people had emigrated. Some went to rebuild England after the war, others were claimed by their relatives in America. Tom Ryan was the local handyman. He was what Gran called 'a business on a bike' because he carried his tins of paints and brushes on the handlebars, and cycled with his ladder slung over his shoulder, whistling as he went.

The rates and ground rent had to be paid annually. Although Bill put by a certain amount each week, he still found the rates a crippling expense. The house was too big for their simple requirements. They lived mainly in the kitchen, cooking and eating all their meals at the scrubbed table, entertaining neighbours and friends, knitting and sewing. Only on rare occasions, when relatives came to stay, did they use the dining-room, with its high ceilings and draughty windows. They would light the fire in the big marble fireplace, but the room was left unused for too long to be comfortable.

It had been a bitter winter, with the cold rising from the hall, seeping up through the rooms. Gran, pulling her shawl over her shoulders, said, 'It's all right for you, Gertie. You don't notice the cold because you're movin' around all the time. Sure, you'd never feel the cold in your own house with so much to be doin'. As for me, I'm treated like an invalid. "Sit down, Gran." "Spare yourself." "Take it easy." "Rest yourself." I'm tired of restin' meself.'

'Wouldn't it be worse if we had you worked to death? Then you'd have a different complaint. Isn't that right?'

Gertie said. 'You still do your share, Gran. Knitting for us all, mending the socks.'

'Which reminds me,' Gran interrupted, 'I must knit John a warm jumper. That thing he calls a sloppy joe isn't suitable for our climate.'

'That'll keep you busy – and there's always the brasses if you're still at a loose end.'

'Not on your Nellie. They haven't been done since Mrs Keogh went to America. They'll wait another while until she gets back. Talkin' of America, any word from Pete, Lizzie?'

Lizzie put down the textbook she was studying for her midwifery exam. 'He'll probably write sometime.' She was determined not to reveal that he had written to her twice – letters full of enthusiasm about Detroit and the motor company where he worked. He did not mention coming home, and she kept to herself the fact that he had invited her out to visit.

'No news is good news,' Gran said.

'He's enjoying himself so much, he hasn't time to write.' Gertie glanced at Lizzie. 'You're still young. Far too young to mope around waiting for the postman, staying in on your nights off. You should be out with your friends, enjoying yourself.'

'I'm not moping around. I have to study.'

Lizzie still blamed her mother for driving Pete Scanlon away. She often wondered what would have happened if he had stayed. Their tentative love might not have withstood her living in the nurses' home in Dublin, only coming home occasionally. He was ambitious and would have become engrossed in his work, no matter where he lived. That time when he had fought in the war was never over for him. It had made him shiftless and erratic. He was too intense about everything. The only consistent thing he had done was to keep in touch with Lizzie.

'Lizzie?' Karen called from her bedroom. 'Will you come up for a minute?'

'Coming.'

Karen was ironing. Lizzie sat down on her bed.

'We haven't had a proper chat since I've come home. What do you think of Hank?' Her voice was excited.

'He's very attractive.'

'He loves me.'

'That's obvious. I'm happy for you. You deserve it.'

'Thanks, Lizzie. I'm glad you like him. I suppose I was attracted to him initially because he reminded me so much of Paul. Except that Paul wasn't obsessed with evolution, and tree-growing.' Her eyes held the same distant expression they had done when Paul went missing.

'Men are usually obsessed with something. With Paul, it was flying. Have they closed the file on him, Karen?'

'No. Of course, I've heard nothing, but his parents had a letter from the Air Ministry stating that, although Paul was missing and by now presumed dead, they were keeping his file open because of the amount of prisoners of war who turn up each year.'

'Supposing Paul's alive? Oh, Karen, wouldn't that be wonderful?'

Karen's face reddened beneath her cream puff powder.

'Of course Paul won't turn up. He's dead.'

'But you just said there might be a chance that he's alive.'

'There might be a chance that some soldiers missing in action are alive. Not Paul. I know,' she snapped. 'Have you forgotten the years I spent looking for him? It was only when I had made up my mind that he was dead that I let myself get involved with Hank. You don't think I'd cheat on Paul? If for one minute I thought there was the slightest chance that he was alive, I'd go to the ends of the earth to find him.' She began to cry, and the old pain of remembering returned.

'Karen, don't cry. I'm sorry.' Lizzie went to her and held her as her slight frame shook with sobs.

'Oh Lizzie,' she wailed, 'I thought you understood more than anyone what I've been through. I'd know if Paul was alive – instinctively.'

'I do understand. If you love Hank half as much as you loved Paul, then he's a lucky man.'

Karen dried her eyes. 'I do love Hank. Oh, I'm so confused. Sometimes when I dream of Paul, I cry in my sleep, and Hank knows.'

'He understands.'

'I guess he does. I mean I suppose so. I'll have to stop

using "I guess" so much. What about Pete? Have you heard from him?'

Lizzie shrugged, and looked out of the window to avoid meeting Karen's eyes. 'He's fine. He's written a couple of times. Still obsessed with cars.'

They both laughed. 'Does he want you to join him?' Karen watched her face closely for a reaction.

'I have no intention of going to America. Anyway, time is a great healer.'

'Who do you think you're fooling? The mention of his name brings a gleam to your eyes.'

'I could never fool you anyway.' Lizzie bowed her head to hide the blush she felt spreading across her cheeks.

'Any word from Vicky?'

'Not recently. The last time she wrote she was thinking of visiting Pete.'

'Did he send her an invitation too?'

'I don't know. She's not the kind to wait for one if she wanted to see him.' Lizzie bit her lip.

'Write back to him immediately. Tell him you'll visit him as soon as you can.'

'Karen, I can't. Mam wouldn't hear of it. Anyway, how could I afford to go? I don't earn enough to save the fare.'

'I suppose you're right. Still, don't leave it too long if you're keen on him.'

'What can I do?'

'You'll think of something.'

2

Gertie sent for Mrs Keogh to help out with Gran as soon as she heard she was back from America. She arrived as Karen and Hank were getting ready to leave. Her bright red curls protruded from beneath her hat, and she was heavier than before.

'How did you like America, Mrs Keogh?' Lizzie asked.

Mrs Keogh pushed back her hat from her forehead.

'Huge,' she said. 'Everything on top of everything else. Them skyscrapers made me dizzy. Me son took me up the Empire State Building. I got sick with the dizziness. We only got halfway up and I couldn't look down. Too many people in New York for my liking. Them huge stores are great, though. Everything you could want in them. Things you couldn't even imagine wanting.'

'How's your husband?'

'He's all right. Comes home when he has nowhere else to go. No thanks to Madge Ryan.'

Although her husband was back home, Mrs Keogh still had not forgiven Madge Ryan for stealing him for a few months.

'That slut.' She spat out the words, showing the pale pink gums of her new false teeth as she did so. 'She got her comeuppance, so she did.'

'What happened to her?'

'I thumped her, that's what I did. Bet her stupid, in broad daylight, when I met her on the street.'

'You didn't!'

'Bet her with me fists. Not once either.' She looked exultant.

'What did she do?'

'What could she do? I had her cornered. She shouted at me to take him back; that she didn't want him. "Take him back!" I roared. "I wouldn't touch your leftovers!" She was terrified, screamed for her mother to protect her. A poor oul wan who was the same age as Gran, I ask you. The coward.' Mrs Keogh pulled lingeringly on her cigarette, savouring the nicotine as much as the telling. 'Do you know, Lizzie Doyle, while she was off cavorting in London, with my husband, I did not have one penny to overtake another.'

'What happened after you beat her?'

'There was a terrific commotion. Everyone shouting at once. Someone sent for the Guards.'

'Were you arrested?'

'Of course I wasn't. Sergeant Mooney knows me well, and is fully aware of the way we served our nation during the Troubles, not to mention our contribution to our community.'

'What did he say?'

'I got off with a caution.'

'What's a caution?'

Mrs Keogh shrugged. 'A sort of warning.' Lowering her voice, she said, 'What he really said was, "Mrs Keogh, Madge Ryan is not worth doing jail for. We all know what a God-fearing, Christian woman you are, and what a fine upstanding family you reared".'

'Mrs Keogh.' Gertie came into the kitchen and stood in front of her. 'You have extra work to do for Gran, not to mention the others, so I suggest you get cracking.'

Mrs Keogh got to her feet. 'I'll manage fine, Mrs Doyle. Hard work is no trouble to me as long as I'm not expected to clean the whole house while I'm attending to the oul one at the same time. I've only the one pair of hands.' She extended her hands for verification.

'We'd never complain about your work, Mrs Keogh,' Lizzie told her. 'We're delighted to have you back.'

'Your work has always been satisfactory,' Mam reiterated, her tone clipped and businesslike. She left as quickly as she came, expecting her departure to bring the conversation to a close.

As soon as she was out of earshot, Mrs Keogh leaned conspiratorially towards Lizzie. 'Your mother's not in the best of form. Is there something up?'

'Not that I know of.'

'Is Karen off again?'

'Yes.'

'I thought so. I hope she gets married soon if that's the case.'

Lizzie laughed into her face. 'Mrs Keogh, she's not pregnant. She's going to Norway with Hank.'

'Oh I see.' Molly Keogh looked disappointed. 'Well, start as you mean to continue I always say, and I'm starting with a nice cup of tea. Will you have one with me?'

'It'll have to be quick. I have to study.'

Adjusting her hat, Mrs Keogh put on the kettle. 'Ah, here's my little treasure!' She held out her arms as John came into the room. 'You've grown so big. How did you like America, pet?'

John shrugged. 'OK, I guess.'

'Listen to him. A real little Yank.'

'Bill says that too.'

Mrs Keogh laughed. 'How did you like your American grandparents?'

'Swell. Grandad took me camping and fishing when Grandma wasn't well.' Thinking of his grandfather made John sad. 'I don't like Hank though,' he said, changing the subject.

'John, you mustn't say that,' Lizzie intervened, but Mrs Keogh waved her hand dismissively.

'It's only the child's innocence. He's speakin' as he finds, as your gran would say. You'll get used to him in time, pet. Now tell me what you find wrong with him.' She watched John's solemn face.

'Darling, go and find out if you can help with the packing,' Lizzie said firmly.

'What do you think of Hank, Lizzie?' Mrs Keogh asked when John had left the kitchen, and the tea was poured out. 'You're a good judge of people.'

'He seems a nice man. A bit self-important perhaps. He's very rich apparently. Maybe that makes him different from us.'

Mrs Keogh took a slurp of tea. 'Thinks he's too good for the likes of us, does he?'

'Not Karen. He loves her, that's obvious. It's also obvious' – Lizzie lowered her voice – 'that he tolerates John for her sake.'

'Oh Lord, that's bad. If your mam and dad knew that, they wouldn't like it. They idolise that child.' She ground her cigarette into the ashtray. 'I'd better make a move, or there'll be nothing done.'

Mrs Keogh sang and clattered her bucket and mop as she worked around the house.

'Less of that noise,' Gran called out to her when she invaded her room with the new vacuum cleaner, twirling it around on the worn carpet.

'This room needs a good turn-out,' she began, lifting Gran's geraniums off the windowsill.

'Leave those alone. I'll see to them meself,' Gran protested, shielding the remaining pots with her outstretched arms.

'They're crawling with maggots. Look at the windowsill. It's rotten with the dirt. Look at the mould.'

'How dare you! I keep me room tidy. And I don't want you touchin' me things. I can never find anythin' when you've gone.'

'Calling me a thief are you?' Mrs Keogh eyed Gran aggressively.

'No I'm not. All I'm sayin' is that I'll do me own room. You'll break the furniture with that Hoover.'

'You're not fit to do it properly. Why do you think I'm here?' Mrs Keogh switched on the vacuum cleaner and off she went again, vacuuming in wide circles to drown out the sound of Gran's reply.

Gran's frail chest heaved with temper. Mrs Keogh stopped suddenly and planted herself in front of Gran. 'What exactly are you missing?'

'Me curlers for one thing, and me hair net. And the good nail scissors I always kept in the manicure set Lizzie gave me for Christmas.'

'You think I took them, don't you?'

'If the cap fits,' Gran wheezed, and winked at Lizzie as she entered the room.

'You've forgotten where you put them, Gran. I'll help you look for them.'

'Lizzie, I don't want her in me room,' Gran hissed. 'I'm entitled to me privacy, aren't I?' Her big eyes looked pleadingly at Lizzie.

'She's blaming me for taking her things.' Mrs Keogh

was breathless with rage. 'Stupid woman,' she muttered.

Gran's room was a mess, with clothes scattered everywhere, drawers open.

'I'll tidy up, Mrs Keogh,' Lizzie said. 'You can find something else to do.'

'Hmm. Wait 'til your mother hears about this. She won't be too pleased. She specified that your gran was my responsibility, and *she's* my employer.'

Karen called out to Mrs Keogh to come and help her close her suitcase, a ploy to distract her from her row with Gran. Mam heard the commotion.

'What's up?' she called from the hall. 'Lizzie, what's going on?'

'I'll be down in a minute, Mam. Gran, tidy yourself up,' Lizzie urged her. She went downstairs. 'Gran doesn't want Mrs Keogh in her bedroom,' she told her mother. 'In fact, I think she'd prefer her to leave altogether.'

'That's ridiculous,' Mam said. 'Mrs Keogh is staying whether Gran likes it or not. We need her help, so Gran will have to compromise. Otherwise, it's a home for her.'

'She's upset that Karen's going away with Hank. I think John reminds her of the time Vicky came over on her own.'

'Well that should cheer her up. She loves remembering when Vicky was here. Anyway, I've more to do than to take any notice of Gran and her vagaries. I suppose we should count ourselves lucky that we have you at home with us.'

'I might not be here much longer, Mam.'

'What do you mean? Your exams are nearly over. You'll get a permanent position in Holles Street. Sister Eugene assured me of that.'

'I don't want a job in Holles Street.'

'You're not thinking of giving up after all that training.'

'No, I love nursing. I need more experience.' She met her mother's gaze. 'I've applied to some hospitals in England.'

Her mother looked around the kitchen at the clock, the vase of flowers, taking comfort in familiar things. Finally she said, 'I don't want you to go to England on your own.'

'I won't be on my own. I'll be living in a hospital supervised by a matron and staff. Only one night out a week, in by eleven I imagine.'

'Well, I'm not happy about it.'

'Mam, I won't come to any harm.'

'Hmm. Look what happened to Karen.'

'I'm not Karen. I won't come home pregnant.' Lizzie jumped up and began pacing the kitchen floor.

Her mother's eyes were on her. 'I suppose you want to get away from here.'

'It's not that.' Lizzie threw up her hands in despair. 'Nursing standards are far better in England. A lot of nurses are going for the experience.'

'You can get that here.'

'It's a well-known fact that hospital work and staff

26

relationships are better there too. For instance, there's a considerable amount to be learned about the care of tuberculosis.'

'I still think—'

'You don't have to put up with what I have to put up with every working day. We're treated like slaves. Docile little nurses at the beck and call of the nuns. Did you know that it's not possible for a nurse to be promoted beyond the position of staff nurse?'

'Why, for goodness sake?'

'Because the hierarchy has the attitude that if nuns are removed from supervisory jobs, the standard of care in the hospitals will drop. The bishops have the gall to think that moral standards will drop too if they're not in charge. It's very frustrating.'

'I'm surprised at you talking about the nuns like that, Lizzie. They do wonderful work and they are God's servants.'

'It doesn't stop them from victimising the nurses. And no one is prepared to do a thing about it.'

'What has made you so bitter about the nuns?'

'It's not the nuns. They're dedicated. It's the slave conditions, I suppose, and the hierarchy in general. Look what happened to the Mother and Child scheme. They squashed it before it could be implemented.'

'Who did?'

'Archbishop McQuaid and the bishops. He wouldn't hear of giving free medical attention to the mothers and children of this country. "The family is dependent on the family," that's his motto. He's not poverty-stricken, though, or trying to bring up a family. If he did a tour of some of the hospitals and saw the real needs, he might be ashamed of living in a palace.'

'You got a good training from them. I'd expect a bit more gratitude.'

'I got a restricted training, and what I got I earned the hard way. Now I want to spread my wings, taste life – see how they do things in other countries.'

'Where else are you planning on going?'

'Wherever the fancy takes me. There's nothing here, only depression and poverty. The hospitals are old and ill-equipped, the standard of care is deplorable.'

'That couldn't be right.'

'Look at the death rate. Infant mortality from gastroenteritis was never higher.'

'Well, you're not lost for words when you want to make a point. You should go into politics. Or join the trade union with your father and Mr Quinn.'

'That's not a bad idea. There should be a nurses' union.'

'You could always start one. God knows you sound militant enough. You've certainly come out of your shell.'

'It's a big, bad world. You should be glad I can take care of myself.'

'As long as you're not bitter.'

'I'm not, and I hate arguments. I'm sorry, Mam.'

Gertie sighed. 'Forget it. Give me a hand with the

sandwiches for Karen and Hank. I've the rashers and sausages parcelled and ready in the fridge. Oh, there's the black pudding as well.'

As Lizzie began buttering the bread, she thought how much she would have liked to talk to her mother about Pete, her other reason for going away. It was time to be sensible about the future. She was afraid that if there was a confrontation with him, nothing would ever be resolved. Perhaps if they met, everything would be all right. Whatever chance she had of seeing Pete again, she would have none with her mother around. She decided there and then to write to him as soon as she had an address in London.

Gran pinned back the squib of hair that had loosened herself from the scrawny knot at the nape of her neck. 'How would a permanent wave suit me, Lizzie? It'd save me twistin' them curlers into me head every night.'

'I don't think a perm would suit you, Gran. Your hair is too fine.'

'Would it burn me scalp? God knows what chemicals they use in them things. Might frizzle me hair completely.'

Karen came downstairs, carrying a pile of clothes.

'The cases are stacked in the hall,' Gran said. 'I can't believe you're goin' so soon.'

'We'll be back before you know it.'

'I'll help you with your case, Mom.' John's whole body shifted sideways as he tried to lift one of the cases.

'It's all right, darling. Hank'll be home soon. He'll take them out when the taxi comes.' Karen opened one of the cases and put in some clothes.

'You'd think you were going for good,' Lizzie said.

John began to cry. Karen put her arms around him. 'You'd hate traipsing around with us. Anyway, Gertie and Bill will take care of you. This is your home.' Her eyes were riveted on him as she spoke. 'I'll write to you every week, and we'll be home in a few weeks.' John nodded.

'You do understand that I have to be with Hank, darling, don't you? He'd be very lonely without me.'

John would have liked to tell her that he would be lonely too, but he knew Bill would be disappointed in him if he whinged.

'That's enough, Karen.' Mam's voice was blunt. 'No need to prolong the agony. You know John will settle in with us.'

Hank arrived back from the town. 'Is everything ready, Karen?' he asked.

'Just about.'

'Too much travellin' isn't good for a child. We'll do our duty by him.' Gran straightened herself and faced Hank. 'He'll want for nothin',' she assured him.

'I know that.' Hank shook Gran's hand, then turned to John and said, 'You'll behave yourself, won't you, John? You won't let your mother and me down by snivelling, now will you?'

'No, sir.' John hung his head.

'A break from your mother will do you good; prepare you for boarding school.'

'What?' John could not believe his ears.

Ignoring his outburst, Hank shook his hand. 'Good man. Chin up.'

The taxi came trundling down the street. Hank took the cases down the steps with the help of the same taxi driver as before.

'Yis didn't stay long,' the taxi driver said congenially to Hank as he slammed shut the boot of the taxi.

'Long enough,' said Hank. 'Come on, Karen.'

Gertie's lips tightened. 'You'd better go. Hank's getting impatient.'

Karen kissed everyone and gave John one last hug before she ran down the steps, waving goodbye.

Gran gazed at the retreating taxi. 'I'm not able for all these goodbyes. One day I won't be here to welcome them home.'

'You'll live forever, Gran,' Lizzie said as she waved until the taxi was out of sight.

As Gertie took John inside, Gran stood staring up at the house.

'What are you staring at?' Lizzie asked.

'I was just thinkin' what wonderful parents you have. Determined to keep the place goin' for John and Karen and all the family.'

The new paint gleamed in the winter sunshine.

'I know. We're overaccommodated when you consider

the terrible housing shortage. Dad has a lot of expense. Still now that they're re-organising the trade union, he might get a better deal at work.'

'Times are very hard. The war took its toll.'

'It certainly did. And we thought we'd got off scot-free. Still we should be grateful. There's many a one homeless.'

3

John often talked to his father. He used a secret voice because his father was not there, and he realised that if anyone heard him they would consider him crazy. Although his father was invisible, John could see him clearly in his mind's eye. He was tall and broad-shouldered, with wing motifs on the left-hand side of his uniform, and stripes on his epaulettes. John was not born when his father had left for the war, but he had seen enough photographs of him to make him real and solid in his mind. His mother had told him lots of interesting things about his father, so that he felt he knew him very well.

Now, walking home from school, he kicked the gravel on the footpath and surveyed tiny ants in the cracks of the pavement. He said to his father, 'Why did Hank have to take Mom away from me? It's lonely without her.'

The voice in his head said, 'She'll be back, little man. It isn't as if you're all alone. You have Bill and Gertie. And Gran.'

'I know. But I miss Mom. The house is quiet and lonely. Gran goes on and on about everything. She gives me a headache. And I don't like my new school.'

The wind through the telegraph wires sighed and John understood that his father was lonely because he was not there with him. He stared up at the sky, his eyes misting over as he watched the storm clouds gather.

'I think it's going to rain,' John said to his father, but instinctively he knew his father had gone.

A week after Karen and Hank had left for Norway, John started in the Christian Brothers School, on Eblana Avenue, Dun Laoghaire. Because he was a new boy, with an American accent and bright American clothes, he was considered different from the rest of the class, and therefore treated with hostility. Each morning he sat in the front row of the classroom silently enduring the taunts and jeers of the other boys, and ducking the rubbers flicked off the ends of rulers at his head. Brother Ignatius, oblivious to the situation, drummed multiplication and long division tables into them, with the cracking of his bamboo cane. John dreaded most the end of the day. Often he was singled out for their amusement. He was attentive in class, and quick to learn, but he soon discovered that these were disadvantages.

'What did ye learn today, Johnnie sucker?' they would call after him. When he only stared at them, Spike Brady shoved him. His eyes whirled, then he said quickly, 'Tables'.

'What's eight sevens? And you'd better know the answer.'

John stood politely, head bent, afraid to look at them. 'Fifty-six.'

'Right. We'll let you go this time.'

They cornered him in the school yard, as they did with all newcomers.

'You'll have to join our gang. For your own sake. We'll protect you.'

'I don't want to join a gang,' John said and ran off.

Today, feeling very lonely on his way home, he decided to treat himself to some sweets from the corner shop with the penny Gran had slipped into his pocket that morning.

'How are you, John?' Mr Dwyer leaned over the counter to tousle his hair.

'OK, sir. May I have a pennyworth of candy, please?'

'What would you like? Honey bees, aniseed balls, liquorice allsorts or all sorts of liquorice, shoe strings, pipes, lollipops?' Mr Dwyer pointed to the dimpled jars.

John's mouth watered. 'Honey bees, please.'

'One, two, three, four, five, six, seven, eight, nine, ten.' John scooped up the gaily wrapped sweets and stuffed them into his pocket.

Mrs Dwyer appeared from the recesses of the shop.

'Hello, John. How are you? I haven't seen you since you came home.'

'I'm OK, thanks.'

'Did you like it in America?' Without waiting for his reply, she said, 'You look wonderful. You'd never get a tan like that here.' She looked at him admiringly, then puckered her painted face as she went to close the door on the draught. 'The weather's awful. You'd better hurry home before it rains,' she advised, squinting up at the sky. 'It's always raining in this bloody country.'

Mr Dwyer was cross. 'How many times have I told you to leave the door open? Business is bad enough without letting the customers think we're closed.'

Mrs Dwyer shivered. ' "Open" is written on it.'

'It puts people off if the door's shut.' Mr Dwyer opened it, letting John out at the same time.

'S'long,' John called back.

'Goodbye, John,' Mrs Dwyer answered. 'Tell your grannie I was asking for her. Tell her the cold has got into me bones.'

The sky darkened. The first drops of thundery rain fell and gathered speed as John hurried home. His dread of meeting the big boys was another reason for his haste. Spike Brady and his gang marched around in menacing groups, terrorising small children. Thinking about them made him quicken his step. Sometimes he felt embarrassed walking alone. If his father were here, he would have a car, and collect him on his afternoons off, like snotty Janet Shaw's father did. It would be a black, sleek car, that smelt of leather seats, and polish, like his grandad's Chevrolet in North Carolina. The other children stared at Janet as she sat in the back chewing sweets. They wanted to break her pretty neck, and wipe the smugness from her haughty face forever. It would be different with John. His father would offer them all a lift home, and they would be his friends for life.

Theirs was a brightly painted house in a row of dreary houses. As he ran down the basement steps to its sanctuary, he called in to Gertie, 'I'm home'.

The word 'home' reverberated around the silent house, and echoed back to him. John unclasped the straps of his school bag and dropped it on the floor. He ran into the kitchen calling 'I'm home' again.

The kitchen was empty. A freshly baked cake sat on a cooling rack in the middle of the scrubbed table.

Where was everyone? He clambered upstairs calling 'Gran' and 'Gertie' alternately, and almost broke down Gran's bedroom door in his haste to find her. The bed was neatly made, but there was no sign of Gran. He went downstairs slowly, and sat slumped on the bottom step, his head in his hands, his heart filled with fear. It was the first time in his life that he had come home to an empty house.

'Ha. Caught you.'

John leapt up. He found himself confronted by a lanky boy with red-rimmed eyes and greasy hair, dressed in hand-me-downs.

'Who are you?' John's face crumpled with fear.

'Wouldn't you like to know?' Lankyboy curled his lip in a sneer.

'Sure I w-would.'

'You a Yank?'

'No.'

'You sound like them cowboys.'

'Who are you? Where's everyone?'

'Relax. Look at you. You're shivering like an old woman.' He burst out laughing.

'I'm not scared,' John retaliated, in the most robust voice he could muster. He wished he had switched on the light in the dark basement when he had come in.

'We're moving in Saturday,' Lankyboy confided.

'Saturday? Moving in?' John was astounded. 'Where?'

'Here. This very basement.'

'This basement, Saturday?' John was perplexed.

'What are you? A bloody parrot? That's what I said. Self-contained too.'

'Self-contained?'

'Yeh, parrot. Self-contained. That's what they call it when you can close the door on the other nosy tenants. See that door.' He pointed to the door at the top of the stairs with his free hand. 'It's a door, isn't it?' His voice was contemptuous.

John wished he could talk to his father again, but fear numbed his awareness, confusing him. He could not recall anyone telling him that this boy, who had invaded his home, was coming to live in their basement. The effort of trying to remember, and Lankyboy's hand clamped on his arm, gave him a terrifying pain. Suddenly it occurred to him that Gran might have been kidnapped.

'Where are Gran and Gertie?'

Lankyboy released him so suddenly he almost collapsed.

'They went away. They won't be back. You'll read it in the papers tomorrow.' Lankyboy laughed.

'Where?'

Lankyboy splayed his hands across John's face. 'Wait and see,' he grinned, displaying a mouthful of green teeth. 'It'll be on the news. You have a wireless, doesn't you?'

John stepped backwards and fell. As he hit the ground, he felt he was dreaming. But it wasn't a dream because Lankyboy was talking again.

'I'm only codding you. Come on, get up.' He helped him to his feet. 'You're not afraid of me are you?' He peered into John's eyes.

'No,' John stammered.

'When we come to live in your basement, my dad better not find you down here. If you don't stay at the top of the stairs behind that door, he'll kick your backside in.' He lowered his voice. 'The whole neighbourhood was scared of him where we lived before. He has a strap that length.' He spread his arms wide. 'And that thick.' He expanded the gap between his thumb and index finger as far as he could.

John's knees were shaking. He placed his hand over his mouth to stifle a choking sob.

Lankyboy laughed a short laugh. 'Scared you, have I? Come on, follow me. We're going to explore.'

Without a word, John followed as Lankyboy led the way through the dark passage and out the back door, into the yard. He moved rapidly, his worn shoes hardly touching the ground. He raced up the flight of steps to the back garden.

John held back and crouched behind the basement wall, but Lankyboy ran down the steps. Stretching out his arm, he grabbed him. 'Think you're smart, do you? Nobody gets away from me.' He laughed again and John wasn't sure whether to be afraid of him or not.

'Ah, you're home, John.' Gertie's soothing voice floated down from the garden. 'Come up and meet Mr and Mrs Quinn.'

John hung close to Gertie as she introduced him to a dowdy woman with bushy hair and a crying baby held in the crook of her arm.

'I was showing Mr and Mrs Quinn around the garden, John. They're moving into the basement on Saturday.'

A tall thin man emerged from behind the apple trees, Gran leaning on his arm, as she hobbled along.

'Hello. I'm Mr Quinn.' He smiled at John, who withdrew behind Gertie's skirt.

'It's not like you to be shy, John. Say hello.' Gertie nudged him.

John, staring at the ground, muttered 'Hi'.

'You're a nice little lad,' Mrs Quinn said. 'You can come down and play with Anthony and Patsy when we move in. Where is Anthony? Anthony!' she called and the baby roared. 'Shut up will you,' she shouted at the baby. 'I can't hear me ears with you. I don't know what's come over him, Mrs Doyle. He's usually quiet as a lamb.'

'First time I've heard a peep outa him.' Mr Quinn shook his fist at the baby behind his wife's back.

Lankyboy appeared from nowhere and stood meekly before his parents.

'Where were you?' his father shouted at him.

Anthony shrugged. 'Moochin' around. Having a gawk at everything.'

'Where are your manners? It isn't polite to be gawking at other people's property.'

'That's what you are doing.'

'I'll give you a clip in the ear if you don't watch your tongue. We're going to live here,' his father said.

'Where am I going to live? Somewhere else?'

'Artane if you don't watch yourself.'

'I dun nothing, Da, honest.' Anthony's face was red.

'You didn't say hello to John, Mrs Doyle's grandson,' his mother chastised.

Anthony shot John a warning look. 'I never even seen him, he's that small. Hello.'

'He's nine,' Gran said. 'You'll have to mind him if he goes out to play with you.'

John shivered and turned away.

'It's goin' to rain. Let's go in and have a cup of tea.' Gran took John's hand, sensing his bewilderment, and led him away. His heart was hammering. The others followed.

'Sit down and have a cup of tea.' Gertie went to put the kettle on.

'It's a lovely place.' Mrs Quinn looked around the kitchen admiringly, as she seated herself, settling the baby on her knee. 'Not like the last place we were in. You couldn't swing a cat in it. And you could hear every creak.'

'It's far too big for the three of us with my daughter Karen away, and my other daughter Lizzie going to London soon.'

John's eyes opened wide. 'When is Auntie Lizzie going away?'

'As soon as they have a vacancy for her.' She turned to Mrs Quinn. 'She's a nurse. Wants to get a bit of experience.'

Mrs Quinn seemed unimpressed. 'The young today are all the same. Can't wait to get away, and who'd blame them? There's nothing here for them. I'd go if I was young meself.'

John felt a kick on his shins. Startled, he looked up to see Anthony staring at him. 'They don't tell you nothin' in this house because you're too much of a cry baby,' he hissed. 'You start bawling all over the place when they only go out to the garden.'

42

John's face turned scarlet.

'What did you say?' Gran asked Anthony, adjusting her hearing aid. 'This thing's not workin' properly. All I can hear is hissin' sounds. Wait 'til I turn it up.'

'I said it's lovely cake,' Anthony roared into her hearing aid.

'Anthony.' Mr Quinn glared at him, then turned to Gertie. 'The wife's right. This is very nice and we'll do everything to keep it that way. I'm handy with wallpapering and painting and any little odd jobs around the place.'

'There's nothing he can't do,' his wife confirmed. Anthony sniggered.

When they had finally gone, John said to Gertie, 'Why are those horrible people moving into our basement?'

'They're on the list for one of the new houses in Sallynoggin. Unfortunately, they have to wait for it to be built.'

'Won't that take ages?'

'Six months, according to Mr Quinn. They're decent, respectable people, struggling to get by. I don't think he earns much in that butcher's shop he works in.'

Gran said, 'Mr Quinn is the relics of old decency. We've shopped with him for years. Always gave me the best cuts of meat, and value for money. If he owned the shop, he'd be well off.'

'He trained as a butcher in Canada,' Gertie told John. 'Keeps the best bit of sirloin for Bill.'

'I like lamb's liver meself,' said Gran.

John decided that no matter how nice the parents were, he would keep out of their son's way.

Anthony was fifteen but did not look it. His mother thought it was because he was undernourished. His father said it was due to lack of sleep. He was a wiry young fellow, quick and loose-limbed. His clothes were so big for him that sometimes they seemed separate from his body. He was serving his apprenticeship as a carpenter with Healy's, the builders, and hated every minute he spent under the tutelage of Mr Healy, who cursed all the time and blamed Anthony for everything that went wrong.

The smell of new paint greeted Anthony as he opened the basement door. 'Damn,' he swore under his breath, surveying the patch of white paint on his father's blue shirt. 'The oul man will go mad.'

'That you, Anthony?' his mother called from the kitchen.

'No. It's Jesus of Nazareth. Who do you think it is?'

'Less of your cheek. Where were you?'

'Out.'

'Out where?'

'With the lads.'

'You're never in these days. Yer father'd kill you if he knew. He thinks you're helping me settle in.'

'Sure he's never here either.'

'If he finds out you're roaming the streets with that gang of troublemakers, he'll belt you.'

'How'll he find out? Who'll tell him?' Anthony pushed his face defiantly into his mother's.

'I'll tell him.'

Anthony considered the logic of that remark for a second. 'Ah you wouldn't, Ma,' he said placatingly. 'You said yourself that you'd hate to see him lay a hand on me. Anyway, there's a few jobs you want me to do. That's why I came home early.'

His mother glanced at the clock. 'You call this early. It's ten to seven.'

Anthony ignored her. The baby began to cry, and his mother picked him up. 'Can't have him making too much noise.'

'We're paying the rent, aren't we?'

'They're nice people and I wouldn't like upsetting them. That Aga is a godsend. A bit of heat and comfort while you're cooking. Take the clinkers out first thing in the morning, Anthony, will you?'

Anthony made a pot of tea, and poured out a cup for them both.

'You're a good boy at heart.' She took the cup of tea gratefully.

'When's Patsy coming home?'

'Tomorrow I suppose. Your Auntie Maureen wanted to keep her a bit longer in case this place was damp or too cold for her, but I told her it was lovely and warm.'

'Yeh. She should be all right here.' Anthony looked around the room. 'Maybe she'll get rid of her cough.'

'Please God and his Divine Mother.'

'What jobs do you want me to do?'

'So you think if you make yourself useful, everything will be all right with yer da.'

He shrugged. 'Usually works.'

'You're not going out again?'

He slurped his tea, lit two Woodbines, and passed her one. The baby roared.

'Pity the brat can't smoke. I could shove one of these in his gob. That'd shut him up.'

'I'll feed him in a minute.'

'Well, what messages do you want?' Anthony's deadpan voice lifted marginally in an attempt at obsequiousness.

'You're just looking for an excuse to go out again.'

'Sure me da'll be in the pub tonight anyway. It's Friday.'

'As if that made any difference.'

Betty Quinn stood up and swung the baby onto her hip while she poured boiled milk into his bottle. 'I think we'll have a bath tonight, Damien love,' she said to the baby, surveying the tidemark of dirt where she had pushed up her sleeve.

'What's for tea?' Anthony asked.

'Sausage and mash.'

'Again? That's the third time this week. Have you no imagination?'

'You can have a bit of fried bread if you like. There's a lovely bit of fresh dripping in the bowl.'

'Wouldn't you think the oul fella would bring home a bit of sirloin steak for us occasionally. All we ever see is scrag ends and sausages.'

'Don't speak about your father like that. He does his best. Business is bad at the moment. He gets what he can.'

There was a deadness in the silence that followed. Betty Quinn fed her baby, unaware of Anthony's irritation. Her inertia, born out of years of having to suppress her feelings, made her placid. It was useful not to have emotions about anything; she discovered a long time ago that they only caused trouble. She did the best she could. The bit of sewing and darning she took in for Mrs Peterson's large family helped. They were on the housing list, and a baby on the way would guarantee them a house. Betty Quinn might not have feelings, but she was no fool either.

If they got a little house of their own, she could afford the luxury of feelings again. Sallynoggin was a good distance from Dun Laoghaire. Still, they couldn't have everything, and the distance might be a blessing. Keep Anthony out of trouble. He was a good boy really, though a bit high-spirited, Sergeant Connolly had said when he caught him climbing over the back wall of Findlater's shop. Anthony had said that he had heard they were looking for a messenger boy and was going in to inquire

47

about the job. His father said he should have used the front entrance, and skelped him with the strap on his bare backside. The rest of the gang had scarpered. They weren't going to own up to encouraging him to steal.

What about Glenageary Hill? The effort of worrying about pushing the pram up that steep hill, carrying the shopping, getting the children to school, the distance from the shops, gave Betty a pain in her chest. At least they would be warm for the winter here and she would not have to worry about her daughter Patsy's weak chest. She surveyed her mottled legs, burnt from being huddled over the fire in the big damp room they had just left.

Anthony's voice broke into her reverie. 'He doesn't get paid much, does he?'

'No, but as I said he's doing his best. Hope you'll be as good a provider when your turn comes.'

'I'm never getting married. I'm going to travel round the world.'

'They all say that. I said the same. Anyway, things are looking up. Dun Laoghaire Corporation is building homes for the homeless, and your father's joining the trade union movement.'

'Is that a football team?'

She did not answer. In the recesses of her mind she was wondering if her poverty would stay with her forever, like a birthright.

'Come on, Damien.' She took the empty bottle from the baby's mouth. 'We'll get the tea, then I'll bath you.

Patsy'll be home tomorrow to play with you. You miss her, don't you?'

4

She was swinging on the gate when John first saw her. Small, fragile, her tangled curls tied in a raggy bow against her neck. It occurred to him how nice she looked, in spite of her worn coat and down-at-heel boots.

'Who are you?' he asked.

Her eyes roamed over his bright green jumper and blue jeans. 'Patsy Quinn. I live here.' She studied him, head erect, chin out. 'Who are you?'

'John Thornton, and I live here too.'

'You speak funny. You wear funny clothes too.' She put her hand over her mouth and laughed into it. 'Never seen bright green on a fella before. You must be from outer space.'

'My grandma bought me this jumper in the States.'

'States?'

'America, stupid. Never heard of America? AMERICA.' He spelt each letter slowly.

' 'Course I heard of America. We get parcels with them kind of clothes in them from me Auntie Mary, only we won't wear them.'

'Why?'

' 'Cause everyone'd laugh at us. No one wears Yankee clothes. They're horrible.'

'What do you do with them?'

'Pawn them. Me ma bundles them up and takes them down to Breartons on a Monday. She gets a shillin' on them, more sometimes if there's a big bundle. She doesn't bother claiming them back on a Friday.'

John turned to go. 'How old are you?' he asked.

'Eight. How old are you?'

'Nine. Going on ten.'

'Want to play a game of soldiers?'

John stared at her and then said, 'No thanks'.

'Go on. I didn't mean what I said about your jumper. It's nice. It suits you.'

John ignored her and clumped up the steps.

'I've got lots of soldiers me big brother gave me when I was sick. If you don't believe me, come on in and see for yourself. They're in a box under the stairs.'

John turned at the hall door. 'What kind of soldiers?'

'What kind do you think? Toy soldiers.'

'Bring them out to the back garden if you want to play.'

'I'm not allowed in your back garden.'

'Who said?'

'Mammy.'

'You can come if I say so. It's my garden.'

'Oh really?' Patsy tilted her nose with her finger.

51

'What I mean is that I'm the only one who plays in it.'

She looked doubtfully at the house, then said, 'All right, I'll get them'.

The back garden was John's territory. If he was playing Cowboys and Indians, he used the whole reach of the garden down as far as the coach house, racing amid the trees and bushes, aiming his six-shooter at the trees, imagining them as the enemy. Sometimes he climbed the wall at the bottom and looked out at the stretches of fields past Meaney's farm. He would shoot at the grazing cows, pretending to be a cowhand, roaming among his cattle on horseback, lassoing them into order, as he had seen them do in the movies.

Patsy came up from the basement, taking dainty steps along the path to the little bridge that led to the back door. John was waiting for her.

'Isn't this nice?' She breathed in the air. 'What's in there?' She pointed to the shed in the corner.

'Toolshed.' John showed her where the hand mower and all the garden tools were kept.

'Why doesn't anyone cut the grass?' she asked, sinking her ankles into it.

'It's too early,' he called back as she followed him along the narrow path, past the neat flowerbeds, where daffodils protruded from the earth. Fronds of wisteria, bursting into bloom, leaned tenaciously against the granite wall that ran along the back of the garden.

'Let's climb this wall.' As Patsy began to shin up the wall, John pulled her back.

'Not there,' he said, pointing to the thorns on the old climbing rose tree. To distract her, he showed her the water tank. 'It'll soon be full of tadpoles,' he said.

She stared at the acrid green slime. 'Ugh, smells horrible.'

'Bill looks after the vegetables.' John showed her the cabbage patch, choked with weeds, and the neglected raspberry canes. 'He'll start working on the garden soon – then I won't be able to race around here.'

'Who's Bill?'

'My grandad.'

'Why do you call him Bill?'

'Because that's what Mom calls him. That's what everyone calls him. And she calls Grannie "Gertie". I guess it's not to confuse my Grannie with my Gran.'

'That's strange.' Patsy, who had by now lost interest in the conversation, moved further into the garden.

In the neglected area at the back, they sat on logs half-submerged by grass, nettles and blackberry bushes, where Smokey the cat was buried. John felt safe within the confines of the garden. Patsy shivered.

'We can play in the coach house if you're cold. It's my hideout.'

They ran along the moss-covered path, past the compost heap, in a side door, and up the rickety stairs to the loft of the coach house.

'This is great!' Patsy marched around the empty room, her boots making a hollow sound on the bare floorboards.

'It's OK.' John was trying to disguise his pleasure at her obvious delight in the place.

There was something nostalgic about the coach house, a place that retained visible proof of the business of feeding and resting exhausted horses. Patsy was suddenly transported back to the days when horse-drawn carriages were the vehicles of quality. In her mind's eye she could imagine the carriages swaying from side to side with the exertion of the horses clip-clopping along the cobblestones. The crinolined passengers daintily alighting, calling goodnight to Giles, or Edmonds, assured that the horses on whom they depended to get them to their shopping expeditions, or to take tea with friends, or drive them along the seafront, would be well looked after by their coachman.

'It's a proper little house. I like the shape of it,' she exclaimed as she peered into a tiny room, where a sink and drainboard ran along the end wall.

'That was a kitchen once. In the olden days the coachman lived here with his family, and they fed the horses through that chute there.'

Patsy looked down the open pipe. 'There's hay stuck in it still,' she said excitedly.

'Probably from hundreds of years ago.' John was trying to impress her. 'There's a bedroom too, look.' He led the way.

Two china dolls with cracked faces lay in a corner on top of a heap of yellowing magazines.

'Who do these belong to?' Patsy lifted one up and sniffed. 'It smells musty.'

'My Auntie Lizzie used to play with my Auntie Vicky here when they were kids. They had the place all to themselves. They painted and decorated it.'

'I don't like dolls,' Patsy declared, tracing the arched eyebrows, the rosebud mouth, the glass eyes, with a dirty finger. She twisted the head around and threw the doll back on the bed. A squeaky 'Mama' came from the middle of the worn cotton dress.

'You're a girl. Why don't you like them?'

'I don't know why. I just don't. If you had a baby screaming "Mama" all day long in your house, you wouldn't want a doll either.' She looked around. 'What a waste. People could live in this place, make a proper home out of it.'

'It's too cold, and it needs to be repaired.'

'You should see where we lived before we came here. This is a palace compared to where some people I know live.'

She hopped and skipped around, then sat down on a threadbare mat in the living-room. 'I'll make a battlefield of the floor,' she said and began laying out the soldiers in neat rows. 'This is the general. He's out in front because he's head of the army. Next come the field marshals.'

She divided the soldiers in half, lining them up with military precision. Some aimed rifles, others stood at arms. She moved them around, laying some on their stomachs. Others fired a toy cannon. 'Infantry,' she explained, her eyes dancing lights. 'The cavalry are on their way.'

Patsy took more soldiers out of the box. They were on horseback, their uniforms much grander.

'Where did Anthony get them?' John lifted them in turn, holding each one to examine it carefully.

'Me granda. I used to love it when Anthony let me play with him. I suppose he gave them to me to shut me up. Anyway, he got fed up with them.'

'OK, let's play.'

'The Charge of the Light Brigade.' Patsy looked inquiringly at him.

'If you like.'

Her excitement was infectious. Soon the soldiers were in mortal combat, with Patsy shouting 'Bang-bang' and John moving his troops rapidly out of the firing line. When the game was over, Patsy placed the lead soldiers carefully back in the box, putting the toy cannon in a compartment of its own.

'Anthony never played with the cavalry,' she said, looking admiringly at their red unscratched coats.

'Why?'

'Dunno. He's strange. He liked the infantry all right, just never bothered with the others.' She gave John a sidelong glance. 'Anthony's not bad really. He likes to act grown-up 'cause he's the eldest – that makes him bossy. He's good underneath.'

John looked doubtful.

'At least he is to me,' Her lip protruded, her eyes daring John to defy her.

'I don't like him. He's a bully.'

'He's only teasing. You'll like him when you get to know him.'

'I don't think so.'

She closed the box and stood up. 'He gave me these when I was sick.'

'What was the matter with you?'

'Bad cold. I'm better now, but I have to go to the doctor a lot.'

'My daddy was in the air force.'

'What air force?'

'The United States Air Force. He was a fighter pilot in the Eagle Squadrons, in the RAF.'

'Did he fight in the war?'

'Yes. He flew aeroplanes across Europe and bombed the Germans. Mom says he was the best bomber pilot ever.'

'Wasn't he scared?'

'I don't think so. Mom says he loved flying and being in the RAF.'

'Does he tell you all about it?'

'No. He's not here. He's missing in action.'

'In a forest somewhere?' Patsy's eyes lit up.

'Yes. Or a hospital or prison.'

'Will they find him?'

'I don't know. Mom doesn't think so because he's been gone such a long time. But I *know* he's alive.'

'Supposing they did find him. Wouldn't that be exciting? Like something you'd see in the pictures.'

'Pictures?'

'Yeh. In the cinema.'

'Oh, the movies.'

'The flicks, as Anthony calls them.'

'It'd be wonderful. Mom wouldn't have to marry Hank.'

'Who's he?'

'My dad's cousin.'

'Don't you like him?'

'I hate him,' John said vehemently.

Patsy shivered and John said, 'Let's play Cowboys and Indians. I'll get my gun and holster.'

They chased around the garden, firing indiscriminately, screaming themselves hoarse. A watery sun lit the tops of the trees as it made its westward descent. Patsy stopped suddenly and coughed. Her whole body shook with the effort.

'Would you like a drink?' John asked.

She nodded. John led her across the bridge, into the living-room, calling to Gran that they had come in because it was getting cold.

Gran put down her knitting and lifted the shuddering kettle off the cooker. 'I'll never get used to this gas thing,' she complained. 'Here Patsy, sit down. Have a hot drink.' She rummaged through the cupboard. 'Cake, or would you prefer a biscuit?'

Patsy's eyes ran along the box that Gran held in her hand. 'Gateaux,' she read aloud. 'I'd like some of that please.'

Gran chuckled. 'You're a clever little girl.'

'Where's Gertie?' John asked.

'She's havin' a bit of a rest. Lizzie is takin' her to the pictures tonight. I forget the name of it.'

'*Gone with the Wind*,' Patsy said. 'We're going on Saturday.'

'Are you now?'

'Patsy was very sick,' John told Gran.

'Were you?'

Patsy shrugged. 'Bad cough. The doctor thought I had—'

'Had what?' Gran prompted.

'I forget.' Patsy blushed. 'Anyway I'm better now, but I still have to go to have me chest examined.'

'You'll have to keep warm. You shouldn't be out in the damp.'

'That's why we came in, Gran.'

'Maybe you should go down to your mammy, love, as soon as you've finished your tea. Will she not be wonderin' where you are?'

'She knows where I am.'

Gran noted with concern the transparent skin, the blue circles beneath Patsy's eyes, her small frame camouflaged by a wad of clothes, her worn-out shoes. For once she was cautious, knowing from experience to be circumspect about any mention of illness. Her eyes were gentle with concern. This was the Gran John loved. When she flew into a sudden, bewildering rage over something trivial, he got frightened. That only happened when she was confused about things. Then Gertie would take her off to bed where sometimes she would stay for days.

'Can John come to the pictures with us on Saturday?' Patsy asked, through a mouthful of cake.

'What'd you say?'

She finished eating, and cleared her throat. 'Can John come with us next Saturday to the pictures?'

'Depends on what Gertie says. Who's us?'

'Me and me friends, Biddy and Annie Plunkett. We go every Saturday.'

'That must be very expensive.'

'Oh no,' Patsy told her. 'We go to the fourpenny rush.'

'How much is that?'

Patsy frowned at her. 'Fourpence.'

That night in bed John told his father all about his new friend Patsy. 'I know you would like her,' he said to his father before he fell asleep.

5

They met in the woods. Banger, Reilly, Spud, Rasher and Anthony. Their voices were shrill, and their high-pitched laughter carried on the wind.

'I'm putting a point on this that'll pierce the heart.' Banger was paring the end of a long stick with a rusty penknife.

It was a Saturday morning and they had gathered to make new bows and arrows. Tough, dishevelled, defiant and half-hungry, they shoved one another playfully, relieved themselves in the woods, spat onto the ground, smoked with hands cupped around cigarette butts, then combed the woods for saplings suitable for taut bows and straight arrows for their game of Cowboys and Indians.

The sun braided the trees with its light as they plunged into the woods, guns pointed, whipping their imaginary horses into action. 'Ride 'em cowboy,' 'Atta boy,' 'Whoo whoo,' they shouted, firing their Colt 45s. Anthony plunged deep into the thicket, until he had spotted his enemy and, aiming his bow and arrow, fired up into the tree.

'Ouch!' The arrow whistled past Rasher's ear and he jumped down on top of Anthony. 'Did you have to get so bloody close? You could've killed me.'

'That's the idea.' They rolled over, then another arrow landed on the ground beside them.

'Reinforcements!' Rasher cried and tore off while Anthony was distracted.

Spud tired of firing his good arrows from his perch in a tree and sat back among the leafless branches to have a smoke.

'Wawawawawawawa!'

Spud peered down through the budding branches to see Biddy Plunkett and her sister Annie tearing through the woods. 'Damn.' He stubbed his cigarette out on the sole of his shoe. She would have to find them. One thing about Biddy: she was guaranteed to ruin a good game.

'Gotcha! Bang, you're dead.' She fired up at him with her water pistol.

Spud jumped down beside her. 'Who told you we were here?'

'Shut up, you're under arrest. Anything you say will be taken down and used in evidence against you.' Biddy pointed her water pistol at the red feathers plastered against Spud's forehead, secured by an old raincoat belt tied around his head.

'Put that down, Calamity Jane. You look stupid.'

'I wasn't looking for you anyway. I was looking for Anthony.'

'You'd never guess.' Spud cupped his hands around his mouth and roared, 'Lover Boy, your mot's here lookin' for you!'

'What do you want?' Rasher shouted.

'We've as much right to be here as you.'

'We were here first.'

'Leave 'em alone.' Anthony appeared. His face was grimy and a few twigs stuck out of an old helmet he was wearing.

Biddy burst out laughing. 'Whata you dressed like that for?'

'Camouflage. Do you know anything? What do you want?'

'Are you going to the pictures?'

Anthony pulled a butt from his pocket and sucked it while he searched for a match. 'Could be. What do you want to know for?'

'Because.'

He stared at her torn dress, the matted plaits, the dirty socks around her ankles, the worn boots. She was always hanging around, calling to him from shop doorways, chasing him up the street, racing after him on her older brother's bockety bike, or flying along on one roller skate, hair loose, coat falling off her shoulders, shoes caked with mud. Now she looked at him with big, questioning eyes.

'We're going,' he said eventually.

Rasher called 'Come on' to Anthony.

The others ran off into the woods. Anthony hung back. 'Come 'ere.'

Biddy went to him. 'We'll be going to the Pav, I think,' he muttered, then ran off after the others.

'What'd he say, Biddy?' Annie asked.

'He said to mind your own business.'

'Wouldn't touch him. He's too skinny.'

'Watch what you're saying, or I'll give you a sock in the jaw. Come on, let's go.'

When they left, the boys gathered together.

'They would have to turn up and ruin the game,' Rasher said when they were tired debating what films were showing in the three cinemas.

Spud said, 'Will you make up your minds, or we'll be queuing all day.'

'I want to see *Gone with the Wind*,' Reilly said.

Banger looked irritable. 'I'd prefer to see *Hopalong Cassidy*. It's a double feature.'

'We'll toss for it.' Anthony extracted a penny from his pocket. 'Heads for *Gone with the Wind*.' He looked from one face to another.

They nodded.

He flicked the coin. '*Gone with the Wind* it is.' He returned the coin quickly to his pocket, and headed for the Pavilion, the others trailing after him.

Biddy and Annie Plunkett lived at the end of a narrow street, in one of a long row of huddled-together houses.

To get to Biddy's house, John and Patsy had to pass women standing on their doorsteps staring at them, or shouting to one another across the street. Biddy, who was fourteen, was the eldest of five children. She slept with Annie and their little sister May in the same bed. Their brothers, Sean and Dennis, had gone to work on the building sites in England.

In the summer they played ball on the street, chanting 'Queenie I Oh, Who has the Ball?', or sat on the curb waiting for their turn at hopscotch. They went to mass on Sundays and sat quietly with their parents, floral dresses darned, knees clean, their straw bonnets tied in big bows under their chins. They raced around the school yard playing tig, drank milk from stout bottles, stole sweets from Woolworths, and tripped up small boys. Their mother fed them boiled bacon and cabbage most days. Biddy had finished in the national school and was hoping her mother would let her go to the Tech to learn shorthand and typing. Meanwhile she minded a baby for Mrs Troy, an English lady who lived in a big house on the seafront, and collected potato skins and leftovers from the neighbours to sell to the Slop man for pig swill.

'Got your money?' Patsy greeted Biddy when she answered the door.

Biddy tapped the pocket of her cut-down coat, her dark eyes fixed on John. 'Who's he?' she asked, eyes glistening.

'John. Lives upstairs.'

'Very posh.' She threw back her long, straggly hair and called into the dark passage, 'Hurry up, Annie'.

Annie came out, slamming the door behind her. She was smaller than Biddy and darker.

'Are you a gypsy?' John asked her.

'I wish I was.' Annie sighed. 'I'd be living in the woods. Wouldn't be stuck with her.' She pulled a face behind her sister's back.

'If we don't hurry, we'll be late,' Patsy called over her shoulder.

They ran through back alleyways, past open doors that emitted smells of stale cooking, down to the seafront, and along by the yacht club. The queue was forming for the fourpenny rush. Their eyes were fixed on the girl in the popcorn kiosk. She was filling candy-striped bags to the brim with fresh popcorn. The smell tantalised their nostrils as they moved forward in the queue.

'I've got a tanner to spend. How much have you?' Annie asked.

John had a shilling, but Patsy only had the price of the cinema.

'That's plenty. Do you want popcorn?' Annie asked.

They wrapped their hands around the hot bags. John did not mind the waiting or the cold. The anticipation of going to the cinema was almost as exciting as the actual event.

'There he is. Yankee boy himself.' Mickey Brown from John's class was pointing to him and, before John realised what was happening, he was surrounded by a group of shouting boys.

'Hello, weakling,' they called. 'Going to the flicks with girls.'

'Yankee boy go home,' someone shouted, and they laughed.

Mickey Brown grabbed him around the waist.

'Leave him alone,' Patsy shouted.

Suddenly John had disappeared beneath a heap of flailing arms and kicking legs.

'Bullies!' Biddy screamed and moved into the fray, head down, pummelling her fists into their backs, anywhere she could get them. Then she fell on top of them, punching and kicking, and screaming, 'Leave him alone! Leave him alone!'

Someone grabbed her hair. She pushed his face back with her open palm, and rolled away from him, to continue her punching and kicking.

'Stop, you cowards, stop it! I'll tell my big brother,' Patsy called, her voice shrill.

Annie opened her mouth and screamed.

Anthony appeared from nowhere. 'Stop!' he roared and the boys rose and moved back, exposing John. He was lying on the ground, blood pouring from his nose. One boy hopped around, holding one leg. 'Oh, me leg. Oh, me leg,' he whimpered.

Anthony ignored him and helped John to his feet.

'I bit him, I bit him.' John was delighted, in spite of the

swelling over his eye that was already distorting his face, and the blood that was oozing from his nose.

'Oh, he's hurt.' Patsy looked very distressed and began dabbing his face with a bit of a rag her mother made her keep in her pocket.

'I'm OK.' John shook her off, but took the rag she insisted he hold to his nose.

'I kicked them too,' Biddy said gleefully. 'I like a good fight. Give us a fag, Anto.'

Anthony was shouting at Mickey Brown, 'It's nothing to what I'll do to you if I ever catch you near John again. Cowards the lot of you.'

The boys ran off, Anthony after them. He caught two of them and bashed their heads together.

'Leave us alone,' Mickey Brown yelled. 'His father is a Guard.'

'I don't care what he is. I'll beat the living daylight outa you if I ever catch you near that young fella again.'

He turned to John. 'Keep away from those gurriers.'

'He didn't go near them,' Patsy said.

'They're in my class.' John retorted.

'Come to me if you've any more trouble with them. I'll fix them good and proper.' Anthony pointed to his own meagre chest. 'Come on, you had all better sit with us in the pictures. Just this once, mind.' He gave Biddy the butt of a Woodbine.

'Thanks, Anthony.' She looked at him adoringly.

'You earned it,' he said grudgingly.

When the doors finally opened, everyone started pushing and shoving. 'Stick with me,' Anthony commanded, jostling his way through the crowds to pay for the tickets.

They followed him down a wide red-carpeted corridor. Photographs of film stars lined the walls. The usherette flashed her torch up the aisle of the cinema, and along the rows of tip-up seats. They sat facing plush curtains. Finally organ music played and the curtains opened on Pathé News.

'This film will be on for hours. Hope you won't want to go to the toilet all the time,' Anthony hissed through mouthfuls of John's popcorn.

'Shhhh.'

The intensity of waiting for the film to begin was almost too much for John. By the time Scarlett O'Hara appeared on the screen, he felt happy and safe in the comforting darkness, sandwiched between Anthony and Patsy. With Patsy's piece of rag still held to his bloodied nose, he forgot about his injuries, and concentrated on the screen.

From then on Anthony and his gang patrolled the Terrace. Soon John's enemies accepted defeat. John began to relax and, when his homework was finished, he went out to play with Patsy on the street. Though the back garden was still the centre of their world, gradually they began to stray beyond it, finding fun in the lane, among the trees, the protection of Anthony making them feel adventurous.

The garden rearranged itself with the full blooms of spring. Daffodils marched alongside bluebells and tulips. On his afternoons off, Bill worked solidly, planting rows of onions, carrots and cabbages, whistling as he worked. John and Patsy plunged through the wet grass on Meaney's farm to watch lambs being born, and saw a newborn calf, the afterbirth glistening on its skin.

When they got tired of Patsy's soldiers, they played war. It was John's favourite game. He would call silently to his father to watch them as they raced across the grass, arms spread out, making spluttering noises, calling 'Dive-bombers, dive-bombers, watch out,' imitating the Spitfires they had seen in comics and on Pathé News.

6

Lizzie left home on a sunny day in March. As the boat to Holyhead ploughed a furrow through the Irish Sea, she surveyed the church spire that rose above her majestic town, until it had faded into the peaceful landscape, and the town disappeared in a blur of mountains. She would miss Dun Laoghaire, and her family. Yet she knew instinctively that her decision to work in England was the right one. Encouraged by her colleagues, she had written to several hospitals and had secured the position in Harefield Chest Hospital, outside London.

At Euston, queuing for the train with the throngs of Irish emigrants, some with only a bundle of clothes tied with string, or a cardboard suitcase held together with a strap, she thought of Pete, her other reason for wanting to leave home. Although she was now qualified, she knew her mother would find excuses to prevent her from seeing Pete if he returned to Dun Laoghaire. She saw the concern in her mother's eyes. She wished they could talk about Pete. Gertie would be deprived of her daughters, a thought which made Lizzie sad. She would miss her voice singing in the distance while she was doing the washing, or the ironing, or laughing at one of Gran's wisecracks, or chiding Mrs Keogh. It made her sad to think how lonely her mother would be. Since Karen and Hank had left, and would be away for a while it seemed, she had lost her spontaneity.

Harefield Hospital used Nissen huts to cater for the war casualties sent directly from the Normandy beaches. The best medical and surgical equipment, and the most distinguished medical staff, had been evacuated there after the war. In spite of the fact that post-war England was bleak, with food shortages, ration books and low morale, Lizzie fell in love with her new hospital. Its restrictions gave her freedom. She loved her tiny room in the nurses' home, and set about brightening it up. Matron, a tall forbidding woman, interviewed her on her first day.

'Nurse Doyle, I'm sure by now you are somewhat familiar with hospital routine.'

'Yes, Matron.'

'You will do three months' duties in each ward to familiarise yourself with our routine. Your duties will take you to every part of the hospital.'

Reading from a list, the Matron said, 'No visitors in your room in the nurses' home. In by eleven pm. One late pass a week gives you an extension until two am. No make-up or jewellery to be worn on duty. No nylon stockings either. Regulation uniform only.'

'Yes, Matron.'

Lizzie settled in quickly. She took the patients' temperatures, checked their blood pressure, her crisp navy and white uniform rustling as she walked among the rows of neat beds. Her popularity with the staff and patients was obvious in their delight at the sight of her, striding through the ward. She was calm with her patients, refusing to let herself move fast, or make a calamity out of a mishap.

Her first assignment was in the unit for the chronically ill.

'If it isn't Lizzie Doyle? You don't recognise me, do you?' A young nurse stood before her.

As Lizzie gazed at her, authoritative in her staff nurse's cap, it slowly dawned on her that she was looking at Sadie Martin, Karen's bridesmaid.

'Sadie! I didn't know you worked here. How is it I haven't come across you until now?'

'I'm just back from my holidays. Karen didn't tell me you were qualified.'

'She's too caught up in her own life to think about anything else at the moment.'

'How is she? I haven't heard from her in ages. Any word of Paul?'

'No. He's still missing.'

'I have a poor man in the ward who is somebody's son or husband. Rants on about the war. He's probably missing, presumed dead too.'

'Can't they locate his family?'

Sadie shook her head. 'He's been here a long time. Had no identification on him when he was admitted. He reminds me of Paul. I was with Karen the night she met Paul. He was gorgeous. Talk about love at first sight!'

'Karen's engaged to Hank, Paul's cousin. He's good-looking too, but he hasn't Paul's personality.'

'Will they get married?'

'Yes. Karen seems happy enough. It's John who is suffering. Hank isn't his favourite.'

'Poor mite. Karen sent me a photograph of him last year. He's a beautiful child.'

'Tell me about yourself, Sadie. What have you been doing?'

'I worked for the WVS during the raids. Boy, did we have a time of it. We took the mutilated out from under the rubble.' Her voice strangled in her throat with the pain the memory evoked. 'You know, Lizzie, they preached on the wireless about the undefeated British people, about our bravery, how the enemy would never get us down, how we would endure, stiff upper lip and all that. It was a load of rubbish for the press. We suffered, we were on our knees. The women were wonderful. I worked with your Auntie Sissy. She was marvellous.'

'I didn't know you knew Auntie Sissy.'

'Karen introduced her to me years ago. Then we met up again in the WVS. She was fearless. Between air raids she took soup to people, clambering through the rubble and debris, dragging children into the shelters. She was on the go night and day.'

'Mam gave me her address. I'm looking forward to meeting her.'

'I visit her occasionally. She boasts about her precious daughter, Vicky. Between you and me, I think she prefers to forget how little she saw of her when she was growing up. She's very proud of her, takes all the credit for Vicky's achievements.'

'If it wasn't for Gran making those nuns get in a science teacher, Vicky wouldn't have been able to do medicine. Gran was the one who gave Vicky the confidence to go for it.'

'How is your gran?'

'Very well, thank you.'

'She's a marvellous woman. How's Vicky? Have you heard from her?'

'She writes occasionally.'

'You were like sisters.'

'Closer, if that's possible, although there were times when she annoyed me intensely.' Lizzie smiled, remembering her clashes with Vicky over Pete Scanlon.

'Come on. I'll take you on my rounds.'

Sadie led Lizzie from bed to bed, introducing her to each patient, showing her their medical files. Some smiled and spoke to her, others were lost in a world of their own.

'This is Sunny,' she said as they stood beside the bed of

a young soldier. 'Brain-damaged. Reliving the torture he was subjected to in the war.'

Lizzie gazed at the pitiful young man, moaning and writhing in his cot.

'It's all right, Sunny.' Sadie held his hand and spoke soothingly to him. 'We'll make you comfortable in a minute.' She turned to Lizzie. 'When he's sedated, he's calm. Sometimes he cries like a baby though.'

They stood listening to the unintelligible mutterings.

'We christened him Sunny because he smiles when he's tranquil.'

Lizzie took a special interest in Sunny. 'How are you today?' she would ask, and he would always reply 'smashing' no matter how bad he felt, or how deranged he would become in the course of the day. 'You're a sight for sore eyes,' he said to her one day as she was giving him his injection.

He often fell asleep while she sat with him. In repose he looked young and handsome. Sometimes he talked, other times he stared at the walls for hours, or shouted orders. He would sleep like a baby, then wake and groan, wailing and crying.

'When am I going home?' he asked her one day.

'Soon, I'm sure,' she said, holding his hand while she took his temperature. 'Where do you live?'

'Down South.' His brow furrowed with the effort of remembering.

'Are your parents still alive?'

'My mother's alive.'

'Do you have her address?'

'No, I haven't. But she was here yesterday searching for me. I saw her.'

With a sinking heart, Lizzie nodded. 'She'll probably come back again.'

'Yes, I'll wait here for her and I won't leave without saying goodbye to you, Nurse. I promise.'

'I should hope not.' Lizzie lit a cigarette for him and placed it between his lips. 'This is your ration for today, Sunny. Make it last.'

He inhaled deeply, his eyes riveted on her. 'You're a treasure.'

'Is there any way we could find out anything about Sunny's background?'

Lizzie was on night duty with her friend Carol, sitting by the fire, listening to the deep breathing of the patients, the occasional cry of agony, the strangled snoring. Lizzie loved night duty. It was the only time she felt in charge of her ward. She could attend to her patients with more confidence, talk to them without having to watch the time. Nothing interfered with the peace of the night, apart from the occasional emergency. Tonight she was exasperated.

'He must belong to someone. He must be somebody.'

'Nobody has come to claim him,' Carol said. 'We had lots of soldiers like him after the war.'

'What happened to them?'

Carol sighed. 'Some of them died. Others recovered and were sent home when they were eventually identified. Sunny was in a nursing home until he became so ill that he had to go to hospital.'

When Lizzie checked him, he was sleeping peacefully. 'Who are you, Sunny? What's your name?' Only the sound of his laboured breathing broke the silence.

Slowly she walked the ward, checking each patient, before returning to her post.

'I think we give up too easily on them.'

'Who?' Carol yawned.

'The chronically ill. They're defenceless, at our mercy. Then they're shoved off to rot somewhere isolated where no one can see them.'

'After the First World War they shot the poor unfortunates who were gone in the head, or "shell-shocked" as they called it.'

Lizzie was thinking of Paul. Standing at the altar with Karen, proud in his RAF uniform, vowing to love, honour and cherish her, to take care of her for the rest of her life.

'They must have rights.'

'The NHS is doing its best. Unfortunately there's no one to speak out for them.'

The following week Lizzie went to visit Auntie Sissy. A short, stout woman in her early fifties, she came quickly out of the house and down the garden path to greet

Lizzie, her face beaming with pleasure. Lizzie could see what her Gran must have looked like as a younger woman.

'It's lovely to meet you, Lizzie,' she exclaimed, her bright eyes shining with unexpected tears. 'Come in, my dear, come in. You must be dying for a cup of tea.'

'Thank you' was all Lizzie managed to say as she followed the fleeing footsteps of Auntie Sissy into the kitchen, insisting that Lizzie make herself comfortable in her little sitting-room.

The fire was lit. Lizzie sat back into the feather-stuffed sofa. Auntie Sissy brought in a tray laden with sandwiches, cakes and chocolate finger biscuits.

'Well, am I like what you imagined?'

Lizzie looked embarrassed. 'No. It's just that I didn't expect you to look so like Gran.'

'Yes, I've always been told I look like her. That's where the similarity ends. Sorry to disappoint you, Lizzie.' Her brusqueness suddenly evaporated and she laughed. 'You don't have to pretend with me. I know I'm not a great favourite with Mother. We never saw eye to eye. She didn't understand my need to get away. My sense of adventure has got me into more trouble than I'd care to remember.' Her eyes danced with merriment. 'That's not to say Mother isn't a wonderful woman. Don't think for one minute I don't appreciate her, and what she did for Vicky. Of course it was to Bill I entrusted Vicky. I knew I could depend on him.'

'How is Vicky?'

'Wonderful.' Auntie Sissy beamed with pleasure at the mention of her name. 'I have some photographs I must show you.'

She took an envelope from her bag and handed Lizzie the photographs one by one. Lizzie stared at the magnificent girl, trying to suppress the overwhelming sense of relief she felt when Auntie Sissy said, 'This is her boyfriend, Jake, also a medical student.'

'She's beautiful,' Lizzie said enviously.

'Yes, she is. And she's smart.'

It was obvious that Auntie Sissy was putting a lot of effort into making an impression on Lizzie. 'She came first in her class at Christmas. She wants to work in a hospital during her summer holidays to get experience. Just imagine our little Vicky, a doctor in a couple of years' time. If only I'd gotten the chance.'

'You'd have made a marvellous doctor by all accounts. You certainly aren't afraid of the sight of blood.'

'Saw too much of it. You can't imagine what it was like, Lizzie, wading through the debris, searching for bodies. More tea?' she said matter-of-factly.

'No thank you. It must have been horrific.'

'I loved the war. The excitement, the sense of adventure carried me along on a tide of uncertainty. I hated when it was over. The war made us gals feel useful. There was a sense of purpose and fulfilment in my life that marriage and childbearing never gave me.'

'Where did you meet Uncle Hermy?'

'The Hammersmith Palais, nothing more grand I'm afraid. That's where everyone met in those days. Hermy was fine in the beginning. Quite handsome in his own way, and he was different. He had money, bought me presents, took me places. There was a mysterious side to him though. You never quite understood what he was thinking. I found that endearing in the beginning, infuriating later. Then when the war came, he was afraid that if Hitler invaded England, he'd end up in a concentration camp, so he cleared off to Canada. Of course, he wanted me to go with him. Perhaps that's where I made the mistake, because it was when he returned that I realised how much happier I had been without him. I'd been free to do as I pleased.'

'You didn't miss him at all?' Lizzie asked in wonder.

'Those few years of separation made me independent of him. He adored Vicky of course. He wanted more children, but I felt that the times we were living in were too dangerous. One never knew what would happen next. He finally accepted that and was determined that Vicky would want for nothing when the war was over.'

'Why did you go back to him?'

'He insisted that Vicky needed me in Canada. Made me all sorts of promises about a new life, land of opportunity and all that. My Lord, I almost had a nervous breakdown. I missed London, the activity, my friends. Him and his stuffy old family sitting around reliving the "good old days in the old country" nearly finished me.'

'What did you do?'

'I packed my bags and hid them in the spare room. At the first opportunity I left. Vicky understood, gave me her blessing in fact. I think she was glad to see the back of me. She wasn't used to having her mother around anyway, and I knew Hermy and his sisters would take good care of her. He insisted on her staying with him from the time they left Ireland. Said I was flighty, and I suppose I was. Still, why am I wasting time talking about him? Would you like to see the medal I won for bravery?' Auntie Sissy leapt from her chair, almost knocking over the tray. 'I keep it locked in the cabinet,' she said as she extracted a key from a chain around her neck.

'It's wonderful.' Lizzie gazed at the George Cross. The inscription read: 'Awarded to Elizabeth Rosenblume, 1945, for extreme bravery against the enemy.'

'I didn't realise your name was Elizabeth.'

'What do you think Sissy stands for?

'I thought it was a nickname for sister.'

'Your father called you after me because he and I were closer than the others. There's only a year between us. Didn't you know that?'

'No. But I remember that he always stood up for you when—' Lizzie felt herself blushing.

'You were about to say, "when Gran ranted on about you". It's all right, you don't have to pretend with me. Bill was always on my side, even when Hermy came on the scene. Not that he liked him. Accepted him for my sake though. Your dad's solid gold.'

Gran's description of Auntie Sissy bore no relation to this lively woman Lizzie found herself warming to.

'He's the kindest person I know. He accepts everything that comes his way. Especially where Karen is concerned.'

'Poor Karen. Wasn't it awful the way she lost Paul so soon after they were married? I remember when she came back to finish her nursing and search for Paul. Heaven help us, I was afraid she would go out of her mind.'

'It took her a long time to accept that he wasn't coming back. Those poor soldiers I'm nursing remind me of Paul. What gets to me is the fact that they're abandoned. No one seems to care any more who they are. We have a soldier who's dying alone—' Lizzie's eyes filled with tears. 'He must have a family somewhere.'

'What about the International Red Cross, Lizzie? Has anyone contacted them?'

'I know Karen did when Paul first went missing.'

'The Geneva Convention was updated last year and, as far as I know, in one of the Conventions it states that the names of prisoners of war must be given by the capturing authorities to the Red Cross tracing agency in Geneva, so they can visit them and arrange relief.'

'What a good idea.'

'Their tracing agency has been very successful in locating people who disappeared during the war. They did wonderful work arranging for the exchange of family messages, organising reunifications and repatriations. Because they are a neutral intermediary, they gained access to the victims.'

'I wouldn't know where to begin.'

'Contact the British Red Cross first. Their headquarters are here in London. Tell them this soldier you're nursing was brought in from the Normandy beaches. Meantime I'll talk to my friend Myrtle. She worked with the Red Cross during the war. In Paul's case, you would have to contact the French Red Cross because Paul was last heard of in France. I'll ask her to do that if you like.'

'Would you, Auntie Sissy? That would be wonderful.'

While Lizzie was on duty the following night, Sunny's breathing became very distressed. She rang for the doctor, then sat with him while Carol attended the ward. She told him about her visit to Auntie Sissy and the Red Cross tracing agency. 'I'll search for your family, Sunny. They'll come to take you home before you know it.'

He seemed to hear her. His eyes fluttered, his mouth twisted with unformed words. Lizzie put her ear to his lips. 'Th–a–n–k . . .' he began and fell back, his breathing rapid. He moaned, and thrashed his legs.

'It's all right, Sunny, I'm here,' Lizzie whispered over and over. He held her hand in a vice-grip. When the doctor finally came, Sunny was unconscious.

'Pneumonia,' he pronounced, giving him penicillin injections and calling for oxygen.

Sunny slackened his grip on Lizzie's hand and slipped away before the oxygen could be administered. She was inconsolable. The war had deprived him of the basic simple pleasures of living and had taken his life when he was only beginning to live it, without anyone belonging to him knowing. By the time Carol persuaded her to have a cup of tea, her arms were tired from holding him and her back ached. 'If I'd only known about the Red Cross sooner.'

'It wasn't meant to be.'

'He was trying to tell me something and I couldn't understand.'

Matron sent for her. She was brisk and to the point. 'You shouldn't have got so attached to him. You'll have to toughen up if you want to make a good nurse.'

The next day Lizzie was sent to the General Ward. When she came off duty, she phoned the Red Cross.

Two weeks later Matron sent for her. 'Nurse Doyle, I would like a word.'

'Yes, Matron.'

'You seem to have a way with the psychiatric patients.'

'Thank you, Matron. I like them.'

'And they like you. Your efficiency and your optimistic attitude seems to having a calming effect on them. To get to the point, have you ever considered training as a psychiatric nurse?'

'I don't know much about it, Matron.'

'It's a very specialised branch of the medical profession, and would require a certain type of person – someone like yourself. Caring, healthy, strong-minded. Are you interested?'

'I'd have to consider it.'

'Take your time. Let me know as soon as you have made up your mind, and we'll put your training into motion. That is, of course, if you decide to specialise in the field.'

'How long would the training take?'

'A year, initially, in a psychiatric hospital. They're popping up all over the country, and they can't train nurses quick enough. A legacy of the war I'm afraid.'

Later, Lizzie wrote to Pete telling him about Harefield Hospital, the autocratic matron, and meeting Sadie again. She told him about Sunny, about not being able to contact his family because he had no identity. 'Death is all around us, ruthless and unpredictable. It makes me think of Paul. The Red Cross put me in touch with their tracing agency. Wouldn't it be awful if Paul were out there somewhere and nobody knew who he was?' She also told him about Matron's offer to send her to do psychiatric nursing. 'I'll have to think seriously about it,' she wrote. 'I know I would like it, but is that what I want to do for the rest of my life?'

Pete wrote back a month later. A cheerful letter, telling her that he had moved to New York to a new job. He mentioned the bars, the places to go. The deeper, entangled Pete was not evident, and she suspected that he was making a serious attempt at being lighthearted. He finished by saying, 'Now that you've taken your first big step to freedom in this wild, wonderful world, come and visit me and let me show you New York. I would like nothing better.'

7

The absence of Gran's chair, the grandfather clock and the dresser made the kitchen a gloomy place. It seemed darker than John had remembered. There was a damp smell of drying clothes and the Aga did not splutter as much as it used to, or generate as much heat. Betty Quinn saw the surprised look on his face. 'It's choked up. Needs a good clean-out. Awful about Patsy, isn't it?' She gave John a sad smile.

'May I see her, please?' The anxious look on his face made Mrs Quinn look more unhappy.

She shook her head. 'She's in bed, and you can't go in because it's catching. Play with Anthony and I'll make us all a nice cup of tea.'

Anthony was fiddling with the knobs of the bakelite wireless. 'Shhh,' he hissed before John had said anything. '*Dan Dare, Pilot of the Future*'s starting.' When the familiar signature tune began, Anthony settled down to sort comics into bundles, listening at the same time.

'And don't touch them,' he said, eyeing the bundles of

comics. '*Dandy, Beano, Adventurer, Hotspur.*' He read out the names, placing the comics in their correct pile.

'Bill gets me *The Beano* sometimes,' John whispered. Anthony's face brightened. 'Any old copies?' John nodded.

'Bring them down, will you? Me and the gang are collecting them. We're going to sell them to get money for the carnival. If you get me enough of them, I might take you.'

'When?'

'When it comes to Dun Laoghaire, stupid.'

John's lip trembled. Anthony's voice softened as he said, 'Couple of weeks' time. We haven't got long to get as many as we can.' He leaned forward and whispered. 'Buzz off now. I'm listening to this. And don't forget the comics.'

'Come and sit down, John,' Mrs Quinn called.

He watched her pour the tea into brown cups, and cut thick slices of bread from the turn-over loaf, which she buttered and coated liberally with sugar. The baby sucked his bottle in his pram, his red-rimmed eyes trained on John.

'Eat up.' Mrs Quinn pushed the plate in front of him.

While the baby watched, John polished off the hunks of bread, wishing Patsy would appear.

As if reading his thoughts, Mrs Quinn said, 'It's not the same when Patsy's sick. It's hard rearing children. You never know what's going to happen next. Especially in times like these. When's your mammy coming home, love?'

'I don't know. She writes every week, but she hasn't said when exactly she'll be back.'

'You're lucky you've got such good grandparents.'

He nodded. Then, licking the sugar from the sides of his mouth, John said, 'This is lovely.'

Mrs Quinn shrugged. 'It's only bread and sugar.'

'I've never eaten it before.'

'You're joking,' Anthony called over. 'Everybody eats bread and sugar.'

'You were in America for so long, you've probably forgotten.' Mrs Quinn laughed.

John helped himself to another slice.

'I'll tell Patsy you called down.'

'Oh, I nearly forgot. These are for her.' John took a squashed bag of sweets from his pocket and handed it to Mrs Quinn.

'I'll give them to her. You're a good boy.' She rumpled his hair.

'S'long,' Anthony said without raising his head.

As John made his way along the passage, he saw a chink of light from beneath Patsy's bedroom door. He tapped and called, 'Patsy? It's me, John,' in a loud whisper.

Silence. 'Patsy?' He raised his voice slightly.

A croaky voice answered, 'Come in.'

'I can't. I'll sneak down when your mother's out.'

'Just for a minute.'

She was lying in bed weighed down with blankets, her hair tangled on the pillow. Her face was white except for dark shadows beneath her eyes, and red spots on her cheeks.

'Me throat hurts.' She tried to sit up, but collapsed back on to her pillows, overtaken by a fit of coughing. 'The doctor came yesterday,' she wheezed. 'He examined me chest and me throat. Said I'd have to go into hospital.'

'When?'

'Soon as there's a bed.'

'Where?'

'Somewhere in the country. Me Uncle Dick is taking me in his car.'

'I'll come to visit you.'

'It's too far. You'd never be allowed in anyway.' She coughed again. 'Will you mind me toy soldiers for me?'

John looked at the soldiers neatly lined up on the mantelpiece.

'You might want to play with them in hospital.'

'They'd only get stolen. You'd keep them safe.' Another bout of coughing seized her.

John took a silver tin box from his pocket and opened it. Glassies, gobstoppers, steelies and cat's eyes spilled onto the bed. 'Take these marbles. You can play with them in hospital.'

Patsy lifted a big multi-flecked marble to the light. As

91

she gazed at it, some of the sparkle returned to her eyes. She examined the others. 'They're beautiful.'

They heard a key scrape in the lock of the front door.

'Here's me da. You'd better hop it.'

'I'll sneak down before you go if I can,' John whispered as he turned to leave. Patsy's reply was muffled by a fit of coughing.

Mrs Quinn marched into the room. 'How many times do I have to tell you to lie still and not talk?' She turned to John. 'You should know better. Go up home at once.'

'Sorry, Mrs Quinn.' John ran up the stairs.

After her mother had left the room, Patsy lay there, full of self-pity. She shifted her body to make a cooler place in the bed, and did not move after that. She heard her father shouting at Anthony, and the clatter of plates, but no one came to ask how she was feeling. Eventually, when Damien had been put to bed, her mother brought her chicken broth. When she had finished it, her mother rubbed Vicks on her chest in circular movements, with big calloused hands.

'That hurts,' Patsy moaned, moving backwards to avoid the pain.

Her mother ignored her and continued rubbing in the Vicks, then got her to sit up while she massaged the Vicks between her shoulder blades.

'Ouch,' Patsy wailed.

'Hold still,' was all her mother said, easing her movements into a gentle caress.

Patsy, slumped forwards, reminded her mother of a bird with broken wings. 'I'll be back with your cough mixture.' She tucked the blankets in around her.

During the night Patsy vomited, and began to cry because her bed was covered in cherry-smelling linctus, which would make more work for her mother.

'Hush, hush.' Her mother tiptoed toward the bed.

'I'm sorry,' Patsy wept, wanting to stop but unable to.

'Shhh.' Her mother wiped her face with a damp cloth and went to get clean sheets from the clothes-horse in front of the Aga.

The pain eased as her mother's soothing hands wrapped the warm sheets around her. Later, when the coughing woke her again, she felt her mother fussing with the blankets, and heard her coaxing whispers to drink the water she held to her lips. She could feel her mother's love willing her better.

Gertie, Bill, Mrs Keogh and Gran were having their tea when John came in. Gertie looked at the clock. 'You were out a long time. What kept you?'

'I went down to see Patsy.'

'You what?' Gertie looked shocked.

John lowered his head. 'Biddy said Patsy was very sick, so I went down to ask her mother how she was.'

'You were told not to go down there. Don't you realise that her illness is contagious? Now go and wash your hands for your tea like a good boy.'

'She's going to hospital and I might never see her again.'

'Of course you'll see her again. What hospital is it?'

'I dunno. Somewhere far away in the country.'

'All the more reason why you shouldn't have gone down there. Wash your hands thoroughly with the carbolic soap.'

When John had left the room, Gran said, 'God help her. She'll be treated like a leper until she's cured, or worse.'

'Worse what?' Mrs Keogh asked.

'Worse luck that she has to go to Newcastle.'

'The farther the better,' Gertie said. 'She's coughing up blood.'

'That place is badly equipped. No facilities at all,' Mrs Keogh sighed.

'It's the old cholera hospital,' Gertie added.

'That's all changed,' Bill said. 'That doctor who came home from England has done wonders for the place.'

'Who's that?' Mrs Keogh asked.

'Dr Noel Browne is his name.'

'It's killing nearly 4,000 people in Ireland each year according to the paper,' said Gertie.

'Where did this wonderful doctor come from?' Mrs Keogh asked.

'He's the doctor who tried to put through the Mother and Child scheme. He cares about the poor and underprivileged. And with this new BCG vaccine there's hope for the likes of Patsy. Dr Browne is putting money from the Irish Hospital Sweepstakes into extending and improving hospitals for TB patients.'

'He hasn't made much headway with his Mother and Child scheme,' Gertie commented.

'What's that?' asked Gran.

'Free medical treatment for mothers and children under sixteen,' Bill told her.

'That would be a great relief to Patsy's family, and all the other poor people sufferin' in this country.' Gran shook her head.

'He hasn't a hope of getting it through the Dail.' Bill spoke with conviction.

'Why?'

'Because the bishops of Ireland are against it. They say that the right to provide for the health of children is up to the parents, not the state. If you ask me, there's too much interference from the politicians and the church. That oul' McQuaid is very suspicious of Dr Browne. The word "socialist" frightens the life out of him.' Bill scowled.

'You're a fund of information, Mr Doyle.' Mrs Keogh looked admiringly at him.

He perked up. 'I take an interest in what's going on around me. I read the papers.'

'Lizzie says the hierarchy are afraid that if we get a national health service here,' Gertie said, 'they'll lose their grip on the people. Especially if Dr Browne intends to educate the mothers.'

'God knows what he'd teach them,' said Gran. 'Mind you, a bit of education in hygiene wouldn't go astray in some quarters.'

Patsy and her mother were ready when Uncle Dick came to take them to Newcastle in County Wicklow in his old Ford. They did not send for an ambulance because Mrs Quinn could not stand the shame of having to admit that her child had TB, knowing the stigma it would leave on Patsy and the rest of her family.

'Are you all right?' her mother asked as she helped her into the car.

She nodded, but felt angry that her mother was sending her away, and helpless because of her illness. 'I don't want to go,' she had said when Doctor Healy told her mother that their only hope of a cure was to put her into a sanatorium.

'Try and get her into Newcastle,' her mother had pleaded. 'She'd be lost in Peamount. I could get a lift down to see her in Wicklow. Me brother could visit her.'

'They don't usually take children, but if I explain the circumstances, they might stretch a point. I know Dr Browne. He's doing wonders there with his patients. A dedicated man.'

As her uncle drove along the narrow country roads,

Patsy felt more and more miserable. Her mother and her uncle talked in low voices, but she was not listening.

Finally Uncle Dick said, 'There it is, Patsy, over there.'

Through the trees, across the fields, they could see the cream and red building. They drove up a long drive enclosed by a high wall. A nurse met them at the door. Mrs Quinn pushed Patsy forward. 'I'm Betty Quinn. This is my daughter, Patsy. You're expecting us.'

Nurse Farrell looked down at Patsy. 'Hello, Patsy,' she said pleasantly. 'We have a special room for you. One on your very own. I'm sure you'll like it.'

Patsy, too shy to meet her eyes, stared down at the nurse's white shoes. The accumulative pain of heartache and sickness made it difficult for her to breathe. She pulled a handkerchief from her pocket and blew her nose. Her mother put a comforting arm around her.

'You need plenty of rest and care. They'll do things for you here that I can't do for you at home.'

'She'll be all right once she's settled into bed,' Nurse Farrell said.

Her mother gave Patsy a quick hug and ushered her towards the door that Nurse Farrell was holding open. 'Off you go, lovey. I'll be down to see you as soon as I can get a lift.'

Uncle Dick came into the hall. 'Here's your case, Patsy. And here's a few bullseyes for the cough.' He pulled a bag from his pocket and handed it to her. 'Be a good girl now and no whinging.' He looked ill-at-ease as he said to her mother, 'We'd better be off'.

Patsy's lip trembled. 'Thanks, Uncle, goodbye.' Her hug embarrassed him.

Nurse Farrell held her hand and walked her along the corridor. A thin woman in a dressing gown passed them. She stared at Patsy. 'What's that little mite doing here? Don't tell me she's got it too.'

'This disease isn't known for its consideration. Now back to bed, Mrs Forde, so you'll be rested when your husband comes in to see you.'

Patsy was led through a maze of corridors until they came to a brighter, airier part of the building.

'This is the new wing. It's called the Annexe. You'll like it here.'

Another nurse came to meet them.

'This is Nurse Dillon. She'll be looking after you.'

Nurse Dillon was small and pretty. 'Hello, Patsy,' she said. 'Come on and I'll show you to your room.'

'I'll see you later.' Nurse Farrell gave Patsy a reassuring smile and left.

Patsy's room, at the end of a passage, was small, with an iron bed in it, and a glass door leading to a veranda.

'Your very own balcony.' Nurse Dillon opened the door and Patsy followed her out to the veranda.

The sun winked through the trees, casting long shadows on the grass below. Patsy burst into tears.

Nurse Dillon put her arm around her and led her back into the room. 'You'll be all right once you've settled in. When they've done all your tests and X-rays, and you're a little stronger, you'll be able to go to occupational therapy. You'll like that.'

'What's occupational therapy?' Patsy's voice wobbled.

'The patients make cane baskets and tablemats. You could make a lovely basket for your mother. Wouldn't you like that?'

'Yes, I would.' Patsy's face brightened.

'Let's get you into bed, before you get cold.' She helped Patsy undress. 'We'll have to put flesh on those bones. Now hop into bed and I'll tuck you in.' Nurse Dillon unpacked Patsy's few clothes, and put them neatly in the wardrobe. Before she left, she took her temperature.

Patsy was tired from the journey and immediately fell asleep. The evening sunlight poured through her window, lighting up the wall beside her bed, and waking her up. She lay still for a while thinking of her mother and father, Anthony and Damien. Eventually she got out of her bed and walked down the corridor where she stood at the window gazing out at the grounds.

'What do you think you're doing here?' Patsy jumped back and found herself looking into the angry face of a nurse. Patsy stared at her in terror.

'You'll catch pneumonia standing there in your nightie. Didn't anyone tell you you have to be screened first before you can mix with the other patients? Go back to your room at once. I'll be along to take your temperature in a minute.'

Patsy hurried back to her room and climbed into bed, breathless and scared. She lay there with the door open, conscious of the nurses busy in the distance, their voices brisk. She strained her ears to hear what they were saying. Finally the cross nurse arrived with a trolley laden with medical equipment and smelling of disinfectant.

'This is your sputum mug.' She handed Patsy a metal mug with a lid on it. 'Cough into that. I'll take your pulse and your temperature.'

'The other nurse already took it.'

'Then I'll take it again. You must use this bedpan.' She took a bedpan from underneath the trolley. 'You can't leave your bed, not even to go to the toilet.'

Patsy blushed uncomfortably and began to cough.

'Use your mug.'

She reached for the mug and coughed into it. It was a dry racking cough that delivered up a pinkish froth. The nurse wiped Patsy's mouth and examined the contents of the mug.

'The doctor will see you tomorrow. Meantime, I think it's better if you lie flat and don't move. Don't read any of your comics.' She placed a pillow under Patsy's shoulders and tilted back her head.

Patsy fell into an exhausted sleep. The crows

rummaged for crumbs outside on her veranda, unaware and uncaring of her plight. She dreamed about her mother, hearing her voice calling 'Patsy' in her dream. When she woke up, Nurse Dillon was standing beside her with a tray.

'I boiled you an egg for your tea. You'll eat it, won't you?'

'Yes, thank you.' Patsy looked at the pretty traycloth, the buttered bread cut into thin slices, the little dish of jam, and the egg in a Humpty-Dumpty egg cup. She said, 'Thanks, Nurse. I'll eat it all.'

'Good girl.'

The next morning Nurse Dillon told Patsy that the doctor wanted to see her after breakfast. 'I'll change your sheets while you're down in the treatment room. Oh, and you'd better put on a fresh nightie.' She took a nightdress from a bundle of laundry she was carrying and helped Patsy change into it. 'Don't worry. You'll feel better when they prescribe some medicine for you.'

The doctor was tall and grey-haired. He smiled at her and said, 'Hello, Patsy, how are you?'

She looked at him in surprise. 'Sick.' She began to cough as if to confirm her condition.

'We'll soon get you better.' He placed his stethoscope around his neck.

'Mammy says it could take years to get me better.'

'She doesn't know the wonder cures we have here, now does she?'

Patsy shook her head.

'I want you to take deep breaths. In, out. Good. Now deeper. Good girl.' He pressed the cold steel of the stethoscope here and there on her back as she tried to breathe without coughing. Then he examined her by placing his hands on her back and tapping with his fingers, leaning his ear towards her to listen. The treatment room was cold and Patsy shivered. He straightened up. 'Now I have to take a blood sample. It won't hurt you. You're a brave little girl.'

'I don't feel brave,' Patsy said, as he tied a rubber tube around her arm. She turned her face away from him. He rubbed her arm with a swab the nurse handed him, and inserted the needle. Patsy felt a sharp sting.

'All done. Send this for testing, nurse.' He poured the extracted blood into a phial. 'And I want her sputum sent for testing too.' He turned to Patsy. 'Tell me, when did you get sick?'

'Ages ago.'

'Were you sick on and off for a long time?'

'Yes. I had to go to our doctor lots of times. Mammy said it was because of the damp in the house we lived in then.'

'I see. Did you miss much school?'

'Yes.'

'Do you like school?'

'I was the best in the class last year.'

'Good girl. You'll be the best in the class next year too.'

Patsy looked astonished. 'Will I?'

'You will.'

A smile spread over her face and she looked at him as if he had given her an unexpected gift.

'Won't I have to say the rosary all the time to make me better?'

'Not all the time. You'd get too tired. Just now and then. If you do what we tell you, you'll get better.'

'I will?'

'I want you to lie still. No running around, no getting out of bed. Nothing.'

Patsy looked miserable.

'You have to do your share to help us make you well again, Patsy.'

'Will that make my cough go away?'

'I sincerely hope so.'

'Then can I go home?'

He laughed. 'You ask too many questions, little one. Let's take one step at a time, shall we?'

The doctor turned away and spoke to the nurse in a low voice. 'I'm not happy about the right lung. Get the X-rays done as soon as possible.'

Patsy heard him.

Long before Patsy's mother was due, Nurse Dillon gave Patsy a bed bath and brushed her hair. She looked at Patsy's flushed cheeks. 'You're feeling much better today, aren't you?'

'I can't wait to see Mammy.'

'I'm sure you can't. But don't get too excited.'

When Mrs Quinn arrived she looked nervous and worried. She hugged Patsy before sitting down to scrutinise her.

'How are you, lovey? You look a lot better.' Patsy slumped in her bed.

'How are you feeling? Is the cough better? Are you still coughing up blood?' The questions tumbled out, vying one another for an answer.

'It's lonely here, Mammy,' was all Patsy could say.

'Look at your lovely room, and that view of the countryside and the mountains. And all the care and attention. You're a lucky girl.'

'Do they miss me at home?'

'Of course they do. They all send their love. Daddy will be down to see you soon. Anthony sent you these.' She took a few comics from her shopping basket.

'I'm not allowed to read.'

'You will be soon,' her mother said soothingly. 'John has me plagued to know when you are coming home. He gave me these sweets for you.' She delved into her basket again. 'His gran is knitting you a lovely pink bed-jacket. You want to see the stitches she can do. How she remembers the pattern I don't know. She makes it up as she goes along. All the Doyles send their love. Lizzie's gone to England and John misses her dreadfully.'

'Will he be down to see me?'

'They don't allow children. You'll have to write to him when you're better.'

Tears welled up in Patsy's eyes. 'Tell me about Damien. Is he walking yet?'

'Not yet, but he'll be a holy terror when he does. I'll never be able to watch him.' Her mother straightened her bed and Patsy began to cry.

'I should be at home helping you to mind him.'

'Don't cry, love. You'll be home soon, and I'll be glad of the help.' She looked anxiously at her daughter. 'This is the best place for you.'

'That's what everyone says.'

'I nearly forgot. Mrs Keogh gave me a present for you. She made it specially.' She handed Patsy a brown parcel tied with lots of string.

'Oh!' Patsy exclaimed as she unwrapped a rag doll with a mop of red woollen hair, a red patch on each cheek, and a wide curve of a smile. It was the first doll Patsy had ever seen that she liked. 'She's lovely. Doesn't she look a bit like Mrs Keogh? I'll call her Pepper.'

' "Pepper"? That's a queer name for a doll.'

'Mrs Doyle says that Mrs Keogh can be very peppery sometimes and she has red hair too.' She hugged the doll, drawing consolation from her soft body. 'Say thanks to Mrs Keogh. They won't take her away from me, will they?'

'Not unless she gets TB.'

'She looks as if she has it already. Her cheeks are flushed.' Patsy giggled and her mother relaxed in her chair.

'Well if she has, she's—'

'In the right place.' Patsy finished the sentence for her mother.

8

Two weeks later the carnival came to Dun Laoghaire. From St Michael's Church John saw its coloured lights shimmering on the sea and heard the distant, repetitive whine of its music. He ran home to tell Anthony.

Anthony stood with his hands in his pockets. 'Do you think I'm blind? I've seen it for myself.'

'Will you bring me?'

'I'll think about it.' He looked reflectively into the distance.

'Please, Anthony?'

'Don't whinge or I won't bring you. How much money have you?'

'Two shillings. Gran said she'd give me a half-crown when I'm going.'

'That should do. I'll call up for you later.'

'Thanks, Anthony.' John looked almost lovingly at him before he skipped up the steps home.

Anthony called for him that evening. They met the rest of the gang at the corner of Mulgrave Street. Anthony instructed Biddy Plunkett to mind John, so he could walk ahead with the gang. Biddy grabbed John's hand to hurry him along. Annie and her friend Maeve had to run to keep up with them.

'Why are you running?' Annie complained.

'We don't want to lose Anthony and the others.'

'There's no fear of that. You can see them a mile away.'

She was right. They marched along, intent on taking the unsuspecting carnival by storm.

A man with an English accent was holding a loudspeaker to his mouth at the entrance gate. 'Roll up, roll up, for the Hall of Mirrors.'

'How much?' Anthony asked.

'Adults a tanner, thruppence for the kiddies.'

Anthony handed the man his threepence.

'A tanner for you, sonny. The little lad can go in for thruppence.'

'That's not fair. I'm not an adult.'

'You're not a kid either. Next.'

'Keep it.' Anthony was disgusted. 'Come on lads.'

They raced off, Biddy flying after them. John was left alone.

'Do you want to go in, sonny?'

John looked around uncertainly. The gilded red and blue hobby horses caught his eye. They went up and down to the music, nostrils flared, mouths chomped at the bit. He raced after Biddy to tell her about them. She had climbed up to one of the barriers of the dodgems, to watch Anthony and Spud.

'Come on, Anthony. Bash the living daylight outa them,' she shouted.

Sparks flew as Anthony skirted around the rink in his car, then suddenly turned it and headed smack into the oncoming Spud. A cheer went up as Spud's car swung dangerously from side to side, while he struggled to regain control.

'Give us a go, Anthony, give us a go,' Biddy called.

Ignoring her, Anthony called to John, 'Get on board, we'll kill these bums.'

'Get in.' Biddy pushed John into the car.

Spud drew up alongside her and she jumped in. They screeched away, sparks hissing and firing as they tore after Anthony and John. John held on to the seat, rigid with fear. They banged into one another, flinging John backwards and forwards like a rag doll, until he begged Anthony to stop. Finally the cars drew to a halt, and John staggered out.

'Let's have a go on the hobby horses,' Annie called out and they ran over to the graceful horses, who sailed up and down harmoniously, gathering speed to the music.

John gripped his horse's mane. Closing his eyes, he let it take him over hills and through valleys, away to a land of peace, where his mother and Patsy were waiting for him. 'Here I am,' he called to them silently. 'Here I am.' As they slowed down, he opened his eyes to the coloured lights and the darkness beyond them. He felt a surge of loneliness.

Biddy jumped on to the moving platform and climbed up on a red horse. 'Giddy-up there. Giddy-up,' she shouted, slapping the horse's rump with her hand.

The music started up again and the horses soared and dipped, with Biddy shouting 'Ride 'em cowboy' and John yelling 'Faster, faster' as the merry-go-round gathered speed.

'Wouldn't Patsy love this?' John said to Biddy as they went in search of Anthony.

'Why don't you write and tell her all about it?'

'Yes I will.'

When they found Anthony, Biddy gave him a kick on the shins. 'Take me for a go in the Ghost Train, will you?'

A cheer went up from the lads.

'Go on, Ant. I dare you.' Rasher grinned defiantly at him.

'Get lost. I've only got enough dough for the rifle range.'

Biddy took her purse from her pocket. 'I'll pay.'

Anthony shrugged. 'We'd better hurry up then.'

They ran to the train and jumped in. Biddy grabbed his arm, but he shook her off, and sat solemn-faced, concentrating on the tunnel ahead. The whistle blew and they disappeared.

John bought sweets and shared them with Spud. They threw rings at toys, watched a midget do somersaults, and played shove-penny. John's penny landed in the centre of a square and he won a shilling.

'Look, look.' He held it out for Spud's inspection.

'I'll mind it for you.' Spud took the shilling and put it in his pocket.

When John asked for his money back to go into the Hall of Mirrors, Spud said, amazed, 'What money? I haven't any money belonging to you.'

'You have the shilling I won.'

Spud shook his fist at him. 'You little creep. I told you I don't have any money belonging to you.'

'He kept my money,' John complained to the flushed and giggling Biddy when she returned with Anthony.

'Hand it over, Spud,' she said.

'Make me.'

Anthony rushed forward. He grabbed Spud and knocked him to the ground. Biddy kicked him. With a grunt, Spud rolled away and, quick as a flash, was back on his feet.

'So it's a fight you want, is it?' he panted.

They danced around each other in a wide circle, fists covering their faces. Spud moved in quickly to strike with a left blow that drew blood from Anthony's nose. Anthony grunted and staggered. A crowd formed a circle around them. The gang cheered. A frenetic dance began as they punched each other, delivering blow for blow. The blood spurting from Anthony's nose slowed him down as he tried to wipe it away. Spud caught him off-

111

guard and head-butted him. Anthony broke free. Another cheer went up. Anthony pounced on Spud and, with a sudden burst of energy, hit him smack on the mouth. Spud moaned and gasped as Anthony struck him again with a left hook straight into his face. Suddenly Spud's legs buckled under him. He folded over, clutching his stomach in the middle as he sank to the ground.

'Yippee!' Biddy leaped up and down, eyes shining with love for the triumphant Anthony.

'Get up, yellow belly. I'm not finished with you.' Anthony looked murderous as he flung himself on top of Spud.

An official shouted, 'Stop that at once!'

Another man in a top hat grabbed Anthony and pulled him off.

John stood beside Biddy, wishing he could go home.

'Get up,' the man said to Spud, but Spud did not move. He lay still, head lolling, eyes closed, his body limp.

The man leaned over and lifted the lid of Spud's left eye. 'Someone call an ambulance,' he shouted.

Anthony said, 'It wasn't my fault. He laid into me. I had to defend myself.'

'Bit late for that,' the man said. 'Real damage has been done here. You can make your statement to the cops.'

Biddy whimpered, 'He stole that little fella's money. Anthony was only trying to get it back.'

The gathering crowd was silent. The merry-go-round played on, lonely and distant. Finally the ambulance siren whined as it tore into the grounds of the carnival, lights flashing. People moved back. Two men got out, lifted Spud onto a stretcher, put him into the ambulance, slammed the doors shut and drove off again into the night.

Anthony stood dazed and miserable, Biddy by his side. The crowd began to disperse. The music stopped, the lights went out; the magic of the carnival had gone.

On the way home, Biddy said, 'It wasn't your fault, Anthony. Honest it wasn't. You didn't mean to kill him.'

'Shut up, you. I didn't kill him. He isn't dead.' He lit a cigarette and blew smoke into the chilly air.

Rasher nudged him. 'You'll catch it for this from your da.'

'I know.' Anthony moved away.

'Maybe he won't find out.' Biddy looked consolingly at Anthony.

'He finds out everything.'

'Is it true that he keeps his butcher's knives under the bed?' Banger asked.

'Shut up, will you,' Biddy hissed at him.

Anthony walked ahead, hands deep in his pockets. No one spoke. A sad, despondent little bunch trudged home in the dark. It was the first time they had seen the unconquerable Anthony looking vulnerable.

Mr Quinn was so thin that he needed a belt to hold up his trousers, the seat of which was lost among folds of material.

'Damn lock,' he swore in an effort to insert his key. He put his finger to his lips to prevent further obscenities escaping, as sense penetrated his fogged-up brain. It wasn't that he drank every night of the week. Tonight he had earned his couple of pints. He had listened for hours to different members of the trade union movement, trying to digest its history and make sense out of all the speeches.

Mr Quinn was pleased with himself for providing his family with a new home by tormenting both the corporation and the county council for a house in Sallynoggin. He had endured hours of standing in the freezing cold to plead his case to the authorities.

Rubbing his hands together he warmed his nonexistent backside at the Aga. He made a cup of tea, lit a cigarette, and inhaled deeply. Yes, he was well satisfied. His family had never starved. This place was nice and cosy for the winter. His eyes roamed over the ceiling, the walls. No damp patches, and the Doyles were a nice family, proud of their home.

A scraping sound and a bang made him jump. Not that bloody Anthony up to his tricks again. He weaved his way along the passage and quietly opened the door of the bedroom where Anthony was sleeping. His son was snoring gently. He looked at the lump in bed with affection. 'He's going through a phase,' he thought to himself. 'He's not a bad lad really. Must have been the cat making that noise.' Satisfied that everything was all right, he crept into bed and fell into a deep sleep.

Levering himself noiselessly out of bed, Anthony peeled off his clothes, and offered a prayer in gratitude for his salvation. For once he was glad that the drink had rendered his father senseless, saving him from an immediate beating.

The summer had come and Patsy lay still for a long time, hugging her doll, and watching the light play tricks on the ceiling. She dreaded the intrusion of the nurses with their clatter of bedpans, their endless changing of sheets, and repetitive comforting words. She wanted to be left alone to sleep, because the medicine had made her drowsy. Her mother came to see her often, talking about them all at home, rearranging her pillows, making her lonelier than ever. Patsy would hear her anxious questions to the nurses, feel her smoothing her hair, see her eyes dead with suppressed emotion. 'Is it really you, or am I dreaming?' Patsy would say.

'The morphine makes her drowsy,' Nurse Dillon told her mother. 'But she's a lot better than she was.'

Betty Quinn leaned towards her daughter. 'Get well, Patsy, and come home. The summer's here, and you should be out playing with your friends.'

The nurses and staff tiptoed around the bed, tidying

her room. Someone had put a picture of the Sacred Heart on her locker. Christ's hands were outstretched and bleeding, his smile inviting. 'Come to me, and I will give you rest' was written beneath the painting. Patsy did not want to go to him. She wanted to run down to the sea with Anthony and John, to hear the slap of the tide against the rocks, watch the seaweed drift to the shore, its rubbery coils entangling jellyfish, its smell strong on the evening breeze.

She spent most of her day on the veranda, with only the birds rustling in the nearby trees for company. Sometimes, after she had taken her medicine, she would dream of shadowy creatures creeping up to her balcony to scare her to death. Her medicine was given to her several times a day, together with injections that made her drift off into a haze of loneliness.

Once a week she was taken in a wheelchair to the treatment room to have air put in the cavity between her lungs and chest wall. The doctor, waiting to give her an anaesthetic before hooking her to the machine, was always happy to see her.

'How's my girl? Are you feeling any better?'

Patsy's reply was always the same: 'I feel worse.' But he would say gently to her, 'You're getting better'.

Afterwards she felt sick and giddy, with a burning sensation in her chest. One of the nurses stayed with her until she felt better.

'Am I getting worse?' she asked Nurse Dillon one day

116

on their way back from the treatment room. 'Because I feel worse.'

'You're much better. You've put on weight. Soon you'll be allowed up for a little while.'

There was a summer storm. The thunder rolled and the lightning cracked the sky open in a jagged blue streak. Patsy lay in her bed on the veranda, huddled down into the blankets, terrified. If only the nurses would hurry up and take her in. She could feel herself being pulled by hundreds of pairs of invisible hands, trying to remove her from her bed, to take her out onto the roadway, to be mown down by a lorry. The wind rattled the window panes beside her. It blew the rain in gusts against it. She was cold. There was a clap of thunder and Patsy screamed.

Nurse Dillon came rushing out. 'I'm here, love, don't cry. I was just coming to get you.'

The wind blew Nurse Dillon's cap off and tore against her uniform as she dragged Patsy's bed back into the room, bolting the door against the storm.

'You're all right now. I'll get you a hot drink. We're short-staffed and, with Nurse Farrell out sick, it's almost impossible to see to everyone. I'm on my own today.'

Patsy lay still, comforted by the familiar sound of the ticking clock in the corridor, and the drip of a tap in the sluice.

Nurse Dillon returned with a cup of tea and two pink

wafer biscuits. 'I've got a bit of good news for you. You're down for physiotherapy tomorrow morning.'

'Why is that good news?'

'Because it means you're getting stronger.'

The physiotherapist wore a white coat and was small and business-like. 'Hello, Patsy,' she said, looking up from her notes. 'I'm Hilda Green.'

'Hello,' Patsy said nervously.

'Relax. I'm here to make you better.'

'The doctor said that ages ago. I'm not any better.'

Miss Green consulted her notes again. 'The fact that I'm here is an indication that your health is improving. Sit up and we'll see what we can do.'

Miss Green slapped her hands up and down Patsy's back, with the air of a woman fighting a battle. Patsy thought her breathing would stop.

'Don't worry. We'll get your lungs into shape.' Miss Green smiled with satisfaction.

Patsy clenched her teeth.

Gertie heard it from Mrs Keogh. 'They barely made it to the hospital, I believe. Bob Quinn told Mr Treanor, who told Mary O'Shea that Anthony Quinn has the makings of a murderer. The poor lad he bet up is supposed to be on a life-support machine.'

They were in the breakfast room. Mrs Keogh was sorting through a pile of ironing, Gertie was darning

118

socks and Gran was dozing in her chair in the corner, her knitting on her lap.

'I'm sure they're exaggerating. Anthony's a good boy at heart. Very good to John,' Gertie replied without lifting her eyes from her darning.

Mrs Keogh was relentless. 'He has no control over that temper of his. So Mr Treanor said to Mary O'Shea.'

'Poor lad. His father'll kill him.'

'That's if Spud's da doesn't get him first.'

'Maybe he won't hear about it.'

'Not hear about it? In Dun Laoghaire?' Gran piped up from the corner. 'What I can't understand is why you let John out with them. They're a rough crowd when they're together.'

'I thought you were asleep,' Mrs Keogh said.

'How could anyone sleep where there's talk of a murder?'

'It's his mother I feel sorry for,' Gertie said. 'With Patsy in the sanatorium and the baby so cross. And another one on the way.'

Mrs Keogh looked thoughtful. 'She dressed a hard bed for herself spoiling that young fella.'

Gran began to count the stitches on her knitting needles. 'How could she spoil him? That poor woman had nothin' to spoil him with.'

Mrs Keogh looked at Gran with a face that was ready for a fight. 'I'm telling you she spoilt him. Letting him out when his father wasn't around. Giving him money for doing the messages. She turned a blind eye to a lot of things.'

'Quiet,' Gran said. 'I'm countin'.'

Mrs Keogh ignored her. 'Too much freedom if you ask me.'

'There's no use blaming poor Betty Quinn, or anybody else for that matter. Anthony'll be punished for whatever he did. God help him,' Gertie said.

'God help him if anything happens to poor Spud.' Mrs Keogh blessed herself.

'He couldn't be much worse than he is. Lying battered to bits in the hospital.'

'He could be lying in his grave by tomorrow. According to Mrs—'

Gran did not give Mrs Keogh a chance to finish what she was saying. 'It'd be more in your line to say a prayer for the poor lad, instead of all this surmisin' you're doin'.'

'I'll have you know that I've been making novenas since I heard all this.'

'I'm sure you have,' said Gertie. 'I'll put the kettle on.'

Gran folded up her knitting and put it in her string bag. 'I think we'll say a decade of the rosary while we're waitin' for the kettle to boil.'

'Good idea,' said Gertie.

'Start without me,' Mrs Keogh sniffed. 'I have to hang out the washing.' She unplugged the iron and went out.

As soon as she had left the room, Gran said, 'That is the most uncharitable woman I have ever come across.'

'Don't exaggerate, Gran. Mrs Keogh is very kind. Where would we be without her?'

'Better off,' Gran said under her breath and, taking out her rosary beads, began wading through the sorrowful mysteries.

'Why must it always be the sorrowful mysteries?' Gertie groaned. 'There's the joyful and glorious mysteries too you know.'

'Can you think of anythin' to be joyful and glorious about, Gertie? This world is nothin' but a vale of tears.'

'You've plenty to be grateful for. Didn't that horse you backed yesterday win?' Gertie laughed. 'You thought I didn't know that you're good for a few bob.'

Gran blessed herself. 'What about all the ones that I lose on?'

'We never hear about them. I'll have to confiscate your pension book.'

Gran began with the second mystery, the scourging at the pillar.

9

The storm awoke Anthony from a sleep peppered with dreams of faceless doctors, their hands reaching out to grab him for killing Spud, of standing in the dock before a judge, passing sentence. 'Anthony Quinn,' his voice boomed. 'You are found guilty of the murder of Patrick Reilly. You are sentenced to forty years' hard labour.'

Rain hammered beneath his window. Anthony's heart hammered in unison. The storm frightened him. The clap of the thunder and the howling wind, mingled with the voices in the kitchen, were ominous signs to his tormented mind that Spud was going to die. He was cold, confused and afraid. When his father finally came into the room holding a strap, he felt a scream rising in his throat. With great effort, he silenced it. His eyes were fixed on the strap.

'Get out of that bed.'

Anthony leapt out.

'Kneel down.'

The strap flew in the air and landed on Anthony's buttocks. He screamed. Again it cut through the air, and this time Anthony screamed before it made contact with his flesh.

'That'll teach you. No thanks to you he'll live. You bad-tempered little git. If you want a fight, a fight is what you'll get. Not with a squirt like Spud Reilly, though. You're dealing with me now. I'll get you lessons so you can fight proper.'

His father paused, took a deep breath, then lifted the strap to deal Anthony a few more belts.

It was cold, and Anthony had wet his bed. He listened to the rain beating a rhythmic drum against the window pane, as he lay face down on the pillow. He could not move his hips or his legs. Fury ripped through him, and he whimpered into his pillow. He tried to focus on the fact that Spud was not going to die.

There was silence at the breakfast table next morning. Anthony stood while Mrs Quinn doled out the porridge.

'Sit down,' she said, handing him his bowl.

'I can't.' Anthony kept his eyes on his plate.

'He can stay standing,' his father snapped. 'Good enough for him if his backside's raw.'

'How'll he sit down in school?'

Bob Quinn shrugged. 'I don't care, but I'll tell you one thing. He's joining the boxing club. That'll knock the fight outa him, and it'll keep him off the streets.' He pushed back his chair, took his cap from the hook behind the door and stormed out.

'Let's see them bruises, Anthony,' his mother said.

'No.'

'You might have cuts.'

'I'm all right.'

'Don't blame me if you get blood poisoning.'

'I have to go.' Anthony left without another word.

That evening his father came home early and marched him down to the makeshift gym in the Workmen's Club, to join the group of boys who were taking boxing lessons for the first time. He waited while Anthony was weighed by Mr Murphy, the trainer, a heavyset man with a kind face, and a friend of Bob Quinn. His father left with a warning to Anthony to come straight home or else.

'This is no Sunday picnic,' Mr Murphy began when he had assembled the class. 'To become a boxer requires training and skill. You have to be quick on your feet, as agile as a cat, and disciplined. That means being fit. To get fit, you will follow a regimen of skipping, shadow boxing and sparring, every Monday and Wednesday. On Friday you will do running. That should limber you up.'

Mr Murphy looked the boys up and down. 'One warning. Anyone caught smoking inside the gym will be dismissed. Let's begin.' He walked in front of them. 'Stand straight, head erect. That's better.' He stopped in front of Anthony. 'I hear you're a great fighter, Master Quinn.'

Anthony nearly jumped out of his skin.

'Come forward and show us how skilled you are. You can use me as your punching bag.' He handed Anthony a bag full of boxing gloves. 'Get something to fit you out of that and we'll begin.'

Anthony put on the boxing gloves and slowly walked into the middle of the room where Mr Murphy was waiting. The trainer took him by surprise with a swing from the left. 'Come and get me, hands up to your face, come on,' he coaxed Anthony, who boxed at the air, and twirled away each time Mr Murphy came near him.

'You're making no contact; what's wrong with you? I'm here. Come on, hit me.'

Anthony swung at him, and got him on the shoulder. Mr Murphy returned the blow and Anthony sank to the ground. The boys laughed.

Mr Murphy walked to the sideline. 'See. I only tipped him and he crumbled. By the time I'm finished with each and every one of you, you'll know how to fight properly. That's a guarantee. And it's no laughing matter. Every one of you would have been as bad as this fella here. And you think you're great street fighters. I'll teach you how to box. Let's begin.'

One hour later he said to the exhausted boys, 'That's it. See you on Wednesday, at eight o'clock sharp, or you're out. Dismissed.'

'I'll say one thing for you,' he called to the departing Anthony. 'You may not be able to box yet, but you're a lovely dancer.' Someone guffawed. Anthony blushed and walked away.

★　★　★

It was midsummer and Biddy Plunkett was waiting for Anthony outside the Workmen's Club, humming a tune, and trying to look like a casual bystander. Her hair was newly washed and, when she tossed her head casually, the smell of Ashes of Roses wafted on the evening air.

Anthony stepped out of the club, among a crowd of raucous lads, pushing one another aside to get through the door.

'Howayah?' Biddy caught his arm to detain him.

Anthony looked surprised and then angry. 'What are you doing here?' He shot an embarrassed look around him as he moved Biddy to one side.

Someone skitted, 'What do ye think she's doing? Hardly looking for to learn boxing.'

Biddy smiled at Anthony, his presence obliterating any other concerns in her life. 'Haven't seen you for ages. You look strong, broader or something.' Her eyes were on his chest. 'Must be all them exercises.' To see his strength was almost to feel it.

'Shut up, will you.' Anthony's face reddened as he pulled her further away from the entrance.

'What's wrong with you? You've gone all red in the face,' she giggled. She wanted to say something outrageous, but a quick glance at the waiting boys warned her not to.

'What do you want anyway?' he asked again, shifting from one foot to the other. 'I've got to go home.'

'I never see you these days. You're always down here or

126

going off somewhere for a fight. It's not the same any more.'

'What isn't?'

'The gang. They've all sorta broke up.'

Anthony shrugged. 'That's life.' He looked around, uneasy in her presence.

'Will you walk me home?' The bold invitation sent a sharp thrill of excitement coursing through her that she had never felt before. It reached down to her toes.

'I told you I have to go straight home. I'm tired.' Anthony looked at her, then helplessly at the lads who were leaning against the railings half watching. 'Anyway, I'm with the lads.'

'You're always with the bleedin' lads. Keep 'em. Bye.' She walked away, with her head in the air and an exaggerated wiggle of her hips.

'Hey, wait a minute.' Anthony caught up with her. 'I'll meet you outside the church in five minutes,' he said quietly.

'If you're sure it's no bother.' She looked at him with a haughty expression.

'I can't be out too late.'

'I don't live on the moon, you know. It's not that far.'

'Wait at the main entrance. Now go on, skat.' He returned to his scoffing pals with relief and some embarrassment.

'She's after you, Anto. Watch out.'

'Remember what Mr Murphy said about plenty of rest and early nights before the semi-final.'

'Ah shut up. Mind your own business.' Anthony's face was red.

'She's not bad, Anthony. Face like a frying pan, but all right legs,' Spike Brady said.

Anthony raised his fist. 'I'll shove this down your gob if you don't shut it. I'm warning you.'

'What do you think you're doing standing there half naked outside the church, Biddy Plunkett?'

Biddy turned to see Mrs Keogh beside her.

'Devotions are over. I stayed on to do the stations. They'll be locking the church up soon if you don't hurry in.' Mrs Keogh moved towards the street.

'I'm waiting on someone.'

Mrs Keogh looked shocked. 'Haven't you school tomorrow?'

Biddy ignored her, making a silent promise to do the stations if Mrs Keogh left before Anthony turned up.

'Go on home before you catch your death, love. Listen,' she lowered her voice. 'There's dirty oul men going around. You shouldn't be out on your own.'

'Right, Mrs Keogh. Goodnight.' Biddy moved away.

Mrs Keogh caught sight of Anthony in the distance and walked back to Biddy. 'Will you go home like a good girl and save your pure soul.'

'What?'

'The choice between good and evil is ours, you know.'
She eyed the approaching Anthony. 'Here's evil on two
legs if I ever saw it.'

'Anthony's all right. He never robbed a bank nor
nothin'.'

Mrs Keogh looked heavenwards. 'There are other types
of evil.' She eyed Biddy's skimpy dress. 'Things you know
nothing about. Now go on home before you find out,
and tell your mother I was asking for her.'

'Evening, Mrs Keogh,' Anthony said as he came up.

She left without a word to him. He blew a raspberry
after her.

'What did that oul one want?'

' "Biddy Plunkett, you shouldn't be out on your own",'
Biddy mimicked. 'She was advising me about dirty men
and the evils of the world.'

'Oul busybody. She'd know all about dirty oul fellas.
Her husband's always making passes at young girls,' he
said with venom. 'I've had a bellyful of people like her.
Why didn't you tell her to drop dead?'

'Because I like her. What's up with you anyway?'

'Nothing. Let's go.'

On Georges Street, Biddy looked longingly towards
the seafront. 'If you weren't in such a hurry, we could go
home that way.'

'We'll go that way. We'll have to walk fast though.'

They walked for a while in silence.

'I missed you.' Biddy put her hand in his and he left it

129

there, almost as if he had not noticed it. 'How's your da? I haven't seen you since the carnival.'

'His usual nasty self, cursing and blasting us all to hell.'

'Did he beat you?'

Anthony looked into the distance, his eyes evasive. 'It's me ma I feel sorry for. Always making excuses for him. Says he means well. He's all right to her, I suppose.'

'Maybe he does mean well.'

'Does he have to be so hard?'

'Might be for your own good.'

'I hate him. I wish he was dead. When Spud didn't die, I walked around town thinking of ways to escape. I was going to get the boat to England, only me ma found the money I hid under the mattress and talked me out of it. Said I'd get in with the wrong crowd. I'll only stay for another while, see her settled into the new house. Then I'm off.'

'Where?'

'Dunno. I'll find work on a building site. Plenty of work in London.'

'You're under age.'

'That's not a problem. Spud's da will give me a reference, and put my age at seventeen.' Anthony laughed. 'He'd be so delighted to see the back of me.'

'How's the boxin'?'

'I like it. I like it better than working for that fat slob Healy. "Now, Anthony, that's crooked. Now, Anthony, that's not straight. Do your eyes match, Anthony, or can you see at all?" I'd like to become a pro. That's what I'd really like to do with my life.' He blushed, embarrassed by this intimate confidence. 'Do you know that we're the only country in the world to have our own Amateur Boxing Stadium? The Americans don't even have one.'

'You'd be great. Just think, you'd get to travel all over the world.'

'Yeh, punch the hell out of 'em all. Buy myself a bike with me winnings. You wouldn't see me for dust. Might even buy a motor bike if I did well enough. Rev it up outside Mrs Keogh's gate. She'd go mad.' The idea made him laugh. 'I'd shout, "Up yours Mrs Keogh!" and race off. Do a hundred miles an hour along the seafront.' His eyes glazed over as he voiced his daydreams. Biddy did not laugh, and in the telling his fantasies did not seem so ridiculous.

The only world bearable was the one he lived in in his imagination, where his family were unwelcome intruders. He lived for the times when he could be alone to dream his own dreams. It seemed to him that life was a series of chances. It was chance that had taken him to the boxing club, chance that Mr Murphy had singled him out for special training because he was a friend of his father. Now he had a chance of winning his semi-final.

Anthony continued, 'I like the training, the lads, the places Mr Murphy takes us in his truck. Places like Cork and Belfast. I like Mr Murphy. He's a fair man. He's entering me for the National Junior Championships. I could get on a selection team.'

'What's that?

'A team that's picked to play against other provinces, or other countries. I might be picked to play against a British selection team. The boxing promoters go round the various venues talent-spotting.'

Anthony did not tell her that boxing gave him hope, and a sense of purpose, that he did not want to live his life in the same dull way as his father, or the drudgery of his mother. His mind revolted against a life like theirs. Maybe he was born for greater things. If boxing was his only hope of getting out of the rut, then he would give it everything he had.

'Could I have a go on your bike – if you had one?' Biddy's voice jolted him out of his reverie.

' 'Course you could, if you weren't afraid of speed.'

'I'm afraid of nothing.'

'I know.'

They stopped walking and looked at each other. He saw the adoration in her eyes. She wanted to move closer, put her arms around him. She did not want to say or do anything that might spoil this happy state. Better to live in hope that some day he might include her in his plans, than frighten him away for good. Her greatest fear was that he might disappear. He gave her hand a squeeze, and continued walking.

'What do you want to be?' he asked.

'A singer.'

'Didn't know you could sing.'

'I can't, but that won't stop me.'

They had reached the seafront and Anthony stopped to light a cigarette. 'Want one?' He held out the packet.

'A full packet of ten!' Biddy looked amazed. 'Did you win the Sweep?'

'One of the lads who's training for the Leinster semi-final gave it to me because he had to pack 'em in. I have only two a day.' He drew heavily on his cigarette. 'I'm givin' 'em up for good soon.'

'You really do like the boxin'?'

'Yeh. I like other things as well.'

'Such as?'

Anthony turned to her slowly. 'Such as you.'

Biddy blushed. 'Do you really?' She looked at him as if she could not believe what she was hearing.

'That's what I said, and I'm not repeating it.'

Biddy moved closer and Anthony put his arm around her shoulders. She shivered.

Suddenly he withdrew his arm and said, 'We'd better go. It's getting cold.'

Gran waved John off to school, and watched him from the window until he was out of sight. He was dressed neatly in blue dungarees, with a jerkin to match. His shoulders were hunched with the weight of his schoolbag.

'That's a beautiful child,' she said over her shoulder to

Gertie. 'Shame Karen is missin' his growin' up years. She's been gone a long time now.'

'She was supposed to be here last month. When I ask her when she's coming home, she makes one excuse after another. It's that Hank. He has her at his beck and call and he obviously doesn't want to come back. And why should he? John is of no concern to him.' Gertie joined Gran to watch John's retreating figure. 'He's a beautiful child all right,' she said with a smile. 'And certainly growing. He asked for extra sandwiches today.'

John kept his eyes on the footpath until he was out of sight. He ran all the way down Mulgrave Street, but when he reached the town, he did not turn left towards Eblana Avenue. Instead, he lost himself among the morning shoppers. As he queued for the bus to Bray, he kept his eyes fixed on the road ahead, hoping that nobody would recognise him.

'Where to, lad?' the conductor asked.

'Bray, please.'

'Single or return?'

'Return please.'

'Sixpence.' The conductor whistled as John fumbled in his pocket for the money.

The bus left the town and turned right at the People's Park, laboured up Glenageary Hill, and then went past the half-built houses that John guessed was the Sallynoggin housing scheme. Out in the open country it gathered speed, and flew along the road, stopping to pick up a few passengers here and there in isolated places. John sat huddled by the window and stared at the green fields rushing by, his eyes wide with a mixture of fear and excitement. He concentrated on the pleasure of seeing Patsy again. Would she be sick, or would she be much better? He should have asked Biddy to come too. On the other hand, the risk was too great. She might have refused. Worse, she might have told on him. Besides, his money would not stretch to her bus fare and she did not have any. She had said she did not have a farthing.

'Bray. Main Street,' the bus conductor called.

As John alighted, a group of schoolchildren stampeded onto the bus. John stood, his hands stuffed in his pockets, waiting for the Wicklow bus.

The driver of the bus swung the huge steering wheel expertly around the bends of the country road. The open countryside gave John a sense of freedom. He wanted to get off the bus and plunge into the fields, climb trees, breathe in the pure air. The sky was a vivid blue, the sun laced itself through the trees. It was good to be alive.

The bus stopped near a pub. John walked along the damp edges of the grass verge until he came to the hospital's enormous gates. He crept up the avenue like a thief, often stumbling over clumps of grass dotted with daisies and daffodils, until he almost fell into the arms of a man weeding a flowerbed.

'Are ye lost, son?'

John glanced uncomfortably at him and shook his head.

'I'm visiting my sister.'

'Anyone with ye?'

'My mother. She's gone on ahead. I'd better run.'

He ran like the wind, and then stopped, mesmerised by the enormous cream and red building. How would he find Patsy in such a big place? A nurse carrying a pile of sheets came around the corner of the building.

'Can I help you?' She looked kind.

'I'm looking for my sister. My mother's with me. I lost my way.'

'Easy enough in this mausoleum. We'll find your mother, but you'll have to wait here. Children are not allowed in. What's your name?'

'John . . . Quinn.'

When she had gone, John walked in the opposite direction. He entered the hospital through a side door and walked quickly along a corridor. He passed the open door of a room where an elderly woman was having a serious discussion with a nurse. At the end of the corridor he came into a brighter area. Just as he was thinking that he would never find Patsy, he saw another open door, with the sun streaming from it. He peeped in.

'Patsy?'

She was dreaming. The pain in her back and shoulders as she tried to turn cut through her like a knife.

'It's me, John. Patsy, what's wrong?'

'They put air in me lungs today. Blew me up like a balloon,' she rasped. 'It's to make me better.'

'Don't talk if it hurts you.'

The sight of her small body in the hospital bed made John want to cry. She coughed and wriggled to the edge of the bed. Grasping the mug beside her bed on the bedside table, she coughed into it, filling it with mucus. John stood at the foot of the bed, watching as she struggled to get her breath. Finally she lay still, looking at him.

'You'll have to get better, and come home. Anthony is in trouble.'

'What kind of trouble?'

'He beat up Spud. Everyone thought Spud might die, he was hurt so bad. But he's going to be all right. Your father nearly killed Anthony.'

She wasn't dreaming. This was real. John would not make up a story like that. Think, breathe, stop fighting and breathe. Everything hurt, the dull pain in her head and throat. Her arms were numb from injections. Her ribs felt as if they had been sawn off.

'Tell Anthony I'll be home to him soon. I hope he doesn't run away.'

'I will.'

'How did you get here?'

'I got a bus to Bray, and another out here.'

'All by yourself?'

'Yes,' John said proudly.

'Does your mother know?'

'No. I wanted to tell you about Anthony.'

'You'll be in trouble when you get home.'

'They think I'm at school.'

'You'd better get back all the same. It's a long way.' Patsy continued, 'The doctor says I'm much better.'

John looked doubtful. 'It's not the same without you. Anthony isn't allowed out after what happened, and I don't see much of the others. Biddy called one day, but your mother didn't ask her in, so she didn't come back. I don't think your mother likes her.'

'Not if she's after Anthony.'

They heard footsteps.

'That's Nurse Dillon. Quick, hide.'

Panic-stricken, John looked around the room.

'Out there.' Patsy pointed to the veranda. 'Hurry!'

He opened the door and went out just as Nurse Dillon came into the room.

'I thought I heard voices.'

'I was talking to my doll.'

'Not delirious, are you?' Nurse Dillon took her temperature. 'Good. I'll take you out to the veranda soon. It's a lovely day.'

John heard her and crouched further into the corner. A bell rang down the corridor.

'That's Mrs Mitchell again,' Nurse Dillon said. 'What does she want now? I'll be back shortly. Try to have a little sleep.'

Patsy turned her face into her pillow and feigned sleep. When Nurse Dillon's footsteps had died away, she got out of bed slowly and opened the door leading to the veranda. 'You'd better go. She'll be back soon. If you're caught, there'll be murder.' The effort from the exertion of getting out of bed, and the excitement at seeing John again, had left her exhausted.

John had not come home and it was dark. Gertie wandered restlessly around the quiet house. She went over the information she had been given earlier by the Guards. A boy fitting John's description had been seen that morning getting the bus to Bray. Why wasn't he home? He must have missed the bus. Had he been mitching from school?

She paced the room, listening to the rain outside and the roar in her heart. She wished she could go and look for him herself, but the Guards had discouraged her. Why hadn't she realised how unhappy he was? Now she was remembering how much he disliked Hank, how often he had mentioned it, and nobody had taken any notice of him.

As she went to the phone, Gertie was reminded of the time Vicky had run away to London. She wasn't much older than John and she had managed to get on the mail boat all by herself. Thank God Gran was sedated. At least they would not have to listen to her hysteria. She wished she was dreaming – that she could wake up and John would be in his bed. Her head ached. Oh God, she prayed, bring John home safely. It's the end of the world, she told herself, as she dialled the number of the police station.

John ran to the end of the corridor and took the stairs that led to the back of the hospital. He raced across a yard and along a dirt track. The ground grew muddier and his runners got stuck in it. He reached the gate, climbed over it, then went as fast as he could across a field, searching for the road. The sky was dark as he staggered through the woods, his feet and ankles covered in mud. When he heard the sound of running water and came to a wide stream, he got frightened. He crossed it holding on to the branch of a tree, stepping precariously from stone to stone. The ends of his trousers were soaking wet, and when he began running again, his jeans weighed him down. Tired now, he half-walked. By the time he reached the road, he could barely see in front of him.

Eventually he came to a village and went into the grocery shop, where he bought a bag of broken biscuits. He found a bench further down the road, and sat there munching his biscuits, picking out the fancy ones, until he noticed that it was getting dark. There were a few scattered lights in the distance, and John went doggedly towards them, determined to force his legs to keep going. He knocked at the door of the first house he saw with a light in the window.

'Can you tell me please if there is a bus to Bray?' he asked the old woman who answered it, trying not to sound frightened.

'You missed the seven o'clock. The next one isn't 'til nine.'

'What time is it now, please?'

She peered at him. 'It's just after eight. Are you by yourself?'

'No. My mother is waiting for me up the road. We got lost.'

She grunted. 'Bus stop's across the road, in front of that empty house.'

'Thanks.' John walked as calmly as he could to the bus stop.

He leaned on a rusty gate nearby. The wind rose and it began to rain again. Thinking he might be warmer if he waited in shelter, he opened the gate and leaned against the doorway. The door creaked open to his touch. He pushed it further and went inside. As his eyes grew accustomed to the dark, he began to relax.

A burst of lightning lit up the room, followed by a clap of thunder. John crouched in the corner. The thunder rumbled and he hoped he would not miss the sound of the bus coming along the road. His heart thumped and began racing. What if the old shack of a house got hit by lightning, if there was a hurricane? He shivered, pressing himself against the cold wall. The lightning flashed again, fainter, the thunder rolled in the distance, and the rain subsided.

John was exhausted and wished he was in his own bed. Thinking of Pasty and the hospital made him feel sick. She had listened to him, and understood him, but he realised for the first time how ill she was.

If the bus did not come soon, he would be stranded, miles from anywhere. He crawled to the window and watched. Finally he saw the lights of the bus in the distance and ran out to meet it, waving his arms frantically for it to stop.

10

The restaurant in Toronto where Hermy Rosenblume sat waiting for his daughter, Vicky, was warm and he wished he was not wearing his jumper underneath his jacket. Apart from the heat, it made him look fatter than he was. He was conscious of his increasing size when he was in Vicky's company. He swirled the drink in his glass, looked anxiously at the noisy businessmen at nearby tables, and regretted that he had not booked somewhere quieter to entertain his daughter for lunch.

He saw her approach, eyes glittering, mouth smiling. Heads turned to look at her. She kissed him as he half-rose to greet her.

'Hello, father. Sorry I'm late. Do you think I could get a bus? Every one that passed was full.'

'Relax, you're here now. What will you have to drink?'

'Sweet sherry, please. Have you been waiting long?' She sat opposite him, and removed her hat. Her hair cascaded around her shoulders.

'Not long.' Hermy shrugged. 'And how are you, *Liebling?* How's university?' Vicky was a medical student at the University of Toronto.

'Fine. Everything's fine. How are you?'

'Not so bad. The usual pains in the joints. I'm getting old. Mustn't grumble. Is there any point?'

'None whatsoever,' she said, taking the menu he proffered.

'Are you hungry?'

'Ravenous.'

'Have whatever you want.'

Vicky read the extensive menu and sighed. 'I could spend all day trying to decide.'

'We have all the time in the world.'

'You may have. I have to be somewhere at 2:30.'

The waiter came to take the order. 'Let me see,' Vicky said. 'I'll start with the fish soup, then I think I'll have a fillet steak, rare, mushrooms and french fries.'

'Very well, madam.'

'Oh, and a small green salad, please.'

'Certainly, madam.' The waiter bowed and reluctantly turned his attention to Hermy.

'The sole please, and broccoli.' He looked at Vicky and patted his stomach. 'It's my ulcer you know.'

'Lose some weight and you'll be all right.'

'No sympathy for your poor old father?'

'None.'

When the waiter had left, Vicky said, 'What's the occasion?'

'Does there have to be an occasion? Can a loving father not give his daughter a treat once in a while?'

'With you there's always a reason.'

'Why are you so hard on me, Vicky?'

'Years of experience. Now what is it?'

'How did you do in your exams?'

'Fine. That's not why you brought me here.'

'Have you heard from your mother recently?'

'No.'

'Would you like some wine?'

'Father, what's wrong?'

Hermy called the wine waiter, who presented him with a wine list. He began to study it.

'Is there something wrong with Mum?' asked Vicky.

'She's well – considering.'

'Considering?'

Hermy raised his hand. 'Take it easy, *Liebling*. Your mother has not been very well.'

'She didn't mention anything about being ill in her last letter.'

'She probably wasn't ill then.' Hermy ran a finger around his stiff shirt collar. 'She had a heart attack last Tuesday.'

'What?'

'I gather it was a mild one.'

'Is it serious?'

Looking sheepishly at his exasperated daughter, he said, 'She's out of danger now. They kept her in intensive care for a couple of days. You know your mother. She wouldn't stay any longer; wanted to get home to her cats and her plants.'

'Who phoned you?'

'Myrtle. The way she went on, one would think it was my fault. Said Sissy should not be living alone—'

'She could get someone in. A lodger, a companion, a housekeeper if need be. You can afford it.'

'You don't understand, Vicky. She wants to live alone. That's why she went back to London. The woman should never have gotten married. She prefers her own company.'

'Did it ever occur to you that it was you she shouldn't have married? Perhaps she would have liked the company of someone else.'

'Perhaps. The fact remains that she didn't choose to settle down with anyone else. I would have gladly given her a divorce if she had asked me for one, but she never did.'

'She's a Catholic, for God's sake! Divorce doesn't come into it.'

'Yes, of course. I forgot. Still, she has lots of friends. All do-gooders like herself.'

'Be realistic. If she had another attack in the night, her friends wouldn't be much good to her.'

'I agree. That's what I wanted to talk to you about.'

'What?'

'It's not just a question of her being alone. There are other considerations. She needs someone to look after her for a while, though she sounded well and cheerful when I spoke to her. Says the doctor is exaggerating and that the house isn't big enough for a housekeeper – which is true.'

'You mean you don't want to pay someone to take care of her.'

'Nonsense. I offered her anything she wants. That's where you come into it.'

'Me?'

The waiter arrived with Vicky's soup. Hermy remained silent while the waiter served from a tureen. Vicky suddenly realised she was not hungry any more.

Hermy lowered his voice as the waiter left. 'She wants you to spend the summer with her. She didn't say as much, but she implied it.'

'What you mean is that you want me to spend the summer with her.' Enraged, Vicky picked up her spoon and began eating, without looking at her father.

'Keep your voice down, Vicky. She's alone, thousands of miles away. If there was a disaster—'

'You're forgetting that she's in England because she wants to be. It's home. She has a charming little house and her own life. If she wanted to be here with us, she would be.'

'I understand that. Still I'm worried.'

'That makes a change.'

'I know she has friends. But they're friends she looks after, entertains.'

'Fair weather friends you mean.'

'Hangers-on.'

'Exactly. You certainly don't give her much credit, do you?'

'I have no reason to believe that she's a sensible woman.'

'How she chooses to live is none of our business.'

'I'm afraid that's where you're wrong. You're her daughter—'

Vicky put down her spoon. 'So the onus is on me to take care of her?'

'I didn't say that.'

'It's what you meant.'

'Would it kill you to spend the summer with your mother?'

'Quite frankly, yes, it would. I want to earn some money.'

Vicky was thinking of Jake, her boyfriend. In her mind's eye she saw him running through the park, tall, broad-shouldered, skin glowing, teeth gleaming. She had been looking forward to spending the summer with him, swimming and sailing. He was also a medical student, and they had both secured jobs in the same hospital for the summer. Now anxiety about her mother made her furious with Hermy.

'You seem to have a knack for turning my life upside down, always conspiring behind my back. It's been the same ever since I can remember,' she said bitterly.

She was recalling the time she had been sent to Ireland as an evacuee during the war to stay with her grandmother and her cousin Lizzie. She had begged her mother to come with her, crying all the way over on the boat from Holyhead. When she was happily settled in Ireland, her father came to take her back to Toronto, to live with him and her mother, who had become a stranger by then.

'Did you ever consider what I want out of life when you're making decisions for me?'

'Of course I have. Look at you, a happy, well-adjusted medical student. Don't you think I put a lot of thought into that?'

'You never consulted me.'

'You always wanted to do medicine.'

'Granted.'

'I never begrudged you anything money could buy.'

Her father's argument did nothing to improve Vicky's frame of mind. 'You talk about mother as if she were an invalid. She's only in her fifties, for God's sake, and young in her ways.'

'Her heart is bad.'

'If you're so concerned about her, why don't you go yourself?'

'Vicky.' He looked appealingly at her. 'Please keep your voice down. Why is it such a bad idea to spend the summer with your mother? You could visit your relations in Ireland while you're there.'

Vicky was enraged. 'Stop interfering in my life. Changing it to suit yourself, like you always do. I don't know why I bother arguing with you.'

'Are you telling me that you refuse to be concerned about your mother?'

'No. What I'm saying is that this conversation is getting us nowhere. I'm going.'

'Vicky, you haven't finished your lunch.'

'I'm not hungry.'

'Stop acting like a child. Vicky – *Liebling*.'

Suddenly filled with pity for her aging father, she looked at him hunched over the table. Guiltily she said, 'Don't worry about mother. I'll do something.' Exhausted by the argument, she left without eating her steak.

Vicky returned to her apartment full of anxiety. That her mother could have had even a mild heart attack was almost impossible to imagine. Strong, vital Sissy, always involved in some worthwhile project. Perhaps her father was right. It might be the best thing if she were to go over and stay with her for a few weeks. Meanwhile she had to think of the dinner party she had planned for Jake's birthday. She went into the kitchen to make a list of what she needed.

Vicky's apartment was on the ground floor of a large

terraced house with a bay window overlooking a well-kept garden. She had a single, spacious living-room, a bedroom and a tiny kitchen. What little furniture there was had been bought at auctions.

She drew the curtains, then went to the kitchen to prepare the evening meal. As she laid the table, she mulled over the day's events, and wondered how she would tell Jake that their carefully laid plans for the summer holidays were about to come to nothing.

Later, soaking in her bath while the casserole was cooking, she reflected on her life so far, her success at college, her happiness with Jake.

Her mind drifted back to that dreary house her father had bought when they had first moved to Canada, to her parents' self-induced problems, her father's reluctance to let go of his traditional background, and her mother's unwillingness to live the restricted life he imposed on them. Her little pretensions, like living beyond her means because Hermy found it so difficult to part with his money. As far as she was concerned, she had been abandoned by them both when they sent her to Ireland as a child.

It was there that she realised what family concerns were. Ireland, she said to herself, stirring memories of Gran, Lizzie, Auntie Gertie and Uncle Bill. She lay back in the bath thinking of them all. The idea of seeing them again suddenly excited her. She had not thought of them for a long time. She remembered the holiday in the country. Waking up to the cock crowing in the morning. Sneaking out to watch Uncle Mike milk the cows. Collecting the eggs. Drinking lemonade and eating sweet cake in the pub. Saving the hay. She visualised the house in Dun Laoghaire, the terrace full of noisy children. Heard their laughter. Heard Gran's voice calling them in for their tea; felt her arms around her when she cried. Gran must be very old by now. Supposing she were to die without Vicky seeing her again?

Suddenly an idea came to her. What if she were to bring her mother to Ireland for a visit – was there a better place to recuperate? Perhaps her mother would stay there for a while. Her father would pay for everything and she, Vicky, would let him.

Tomorrow she would write to her mother and Lizzie. Already she was outlining her letter to Gran.

As Lizzie rushed to keep her appointment with the tracing agency section of the Red Cross, she felt the first breath of summer in the warmth of the London streets. It was the beginning of May. Lizzie, filled with hope, ran up the stairs of the offices of the Red Cross to be greeted by an attractive man in uniform.

'Hello, I'm Lizzie Doyle. I have an appointment to see—'

'Me.' He smiled at her surprise. 'I'm Keith Clifford. Pleased to meet you.'

Eagerly she shook his hand and followed him into his office.

'Take a seat.' He offered Lizzie a chair in front of a desk strewn with files and papers.

'Now, let's see . . .' He sat at the other side of the desk and drew a file towards him. Something in his expression reminded her of Pete Scanlon.

'We're looking for Fighter Pilot Paul Thornton.'

Hope fluttered and died instantly as he opened the file and Lizzie saw that it was blank. He saw the disappointment in her eyes.

'We have been very successful in tracing prisoners of war. This year's Geneva Convention allows us access to prisons for the first time because we're neutral. So that could be a big help in our enquiries.' He smiled at her. 'Tell me everything you can remember about Paul, and we'll see what we can do.' He unscrewed the top of his fountain pen and began writing.

Lizzie told him that Paul was an American who had joined the RAF early in the war as a fighter pilot, and that he had gone missing when he was flying secret missions. She finished by saying, 'Unfortunately, that's all I remember.'

'Has he any family in the States?'

'His parents are still alive. They live in North Carolina. I can get you their address.'

'That would be a big help and if you could get any information about him from them, anything at all they might have heard during the years he was missing, no matter how trivial, I would be grateful.'

'I'll try.'

'I'm sorry I can't be more helpful,' he said, screwing the top back on his pen. 'But you never know what might turn up. We'll see.'

'He's been missing almost ten years now.'

He nodded. 'It's amazing the amount of people who turn up through our tracing agency, in the most unexpected circumstances.' He looked at his watch. 'I'm finished for the day. Would you like to have a drink with me?'

'I'd love to,' Lizzie said. 'I'm on duty at three o'clock. I'm a nurse.'

'We have time for one. There's a pub around the corner.'

'That would be lovely.'

As Lizzie sipped her drink, she found herself telling Keith all about Sunny, and Matron's suggestion that she specialise in psychiatric nursing.

'You're a caring person,' he said, 'as well as a beautiful one.'

Lizzie blushed as he smiled at her, and she was reminded again of Pete Scanlon. She would write to him when she got back to the nurses' home, and tell him all about Sunny and the Red Cross, without mentioning Keith Clifford.

★   ★   ★

Lizzie wrote to Gertie, telling her about the meeting.

'The best thing to do,' Gertie said to Bill, 'is to write to Paul's family and tell them that Lizzie has been in touch with the Red Cross.'

'Is that wise?' Bill asked. 'Will it not bring back memories they would prefer to forget?'

'If there was the slightest chance of finding Paul, I think they'd be glad to have their memories jogged.'

Bill shook his head. 'It'd be cruel to raise their hopes again, only to have them dashed. Karen searched everywhere after Paul went missing. She'll see this as one of Lizzie's notions or another wild goose chase, and it'll upset her.'

'There's no need to tell her. If nothing comes of it, then she won't be any the wiser.'

'I don't see how anything can come of it. No matter how nice and efficient they are at the Red Cross, they can't find someone who doesn't exist.'

'You really believe Paul is dead, don't you?'

'Yes I do. Otherwise, we would have heard something. Karen is getting on with her life. If they did find out anything after all this time, it could affect her badly.'

'You're at it again, Bill. Trying to protect Karen. When is it going to dawn on you that she's a grown woman?' Under her breath she added, 'Off gallivanting with Hank.'

Bill threw down his newspaper and left the room saying, 'Suit yourself.'

Gertie wrote to Paul's parents telling them about Lizzie's visit to the Red Cross tracing agency, advising them that the agency would be in touch for information about Paul. She did not write to Karen.

11

It was a letter from Pete Scanlon that made Lizzie decide to visit him. It was an upbeat letter telling her about his new job as a car salesman in New York, and the new Ford Sedan that came with the job. The letter ended with a postscript which said, 'Vicky has promised to come for a visit soon.'

It enraged Lizzie to think that Vicky was in touch with Pete and had been invited to visit him. She remembered back to the time when Pete and Vicky were inseparable, before Vicky had followed him to London. The old jealousy washed over her. There and then she decided that she would take up his invitation and go to America. It was Sissy who finally persuaded her that she could afford the trip.

'You have your twenty-first birthday money from your dad and Gran, and some savings.'

'There's very little to spend money on, what with the shortages and having everything supplied in the nurses' home. Just the occasional dance.'

'There you are then.'

'Isn't it a bit selfish to spend all that money on myself?'

'Pete wants you to go. America is very far away and who knows whom he might meet while you're thinking about it. Men are strange creatures. Believe me, I know.'

Lizzie booked her passage with Thomas Cook, and early in September she took the train to Southampton. At the last minute Sissy went to see her off.

'Maybe he'll be disappointed when he sees me.'

'No man would ask a woman to cross the Atlantic unless he desperately wanted to see her.'

'I might be disappointed in him.'

'I doubt it. You've been in love with him ever since you can remember.'

When the last shore calls came, Sissy gave her a reassuring hug before walking down the gangplank. The hooter went, and the tug boats gently led the liner out into the deep water. Lizzie clung to the rails, waving at Sissy, until she was out of sight. She went to her berth, unpacked her nightie and toothbrush, then made her way to the dining room for the first sitting.

The churning of the engine and the roll of the sea made her feel sick. She returned to her berth and lay on the bed. The journey was infinitely slow and Lizzie felt really ill. Each morning she woke to find the liner still ploughing through the endless ocean. She stayed in her cabin, not trusting herself to go anywhere on the ship.

The steward brought her trays of appetising morsels, but she did not touch them. One week later, early in the morning, they sailed into New York harbour, past the Statue of Liberty. Lizzie was overjoyed.

Pete was waiting for her when she came through customs.

'Lizzie!' He held out his arms and she went into them.

She stood looking into his face, remembering his eyes, now made more intensely blue by a tan.

'You don't know how much I've missed you.' Tears welled up in his eyes. 'It's so good to see you.' He hugged her. 'I thought you'd never get here.'

'There were times when I thought that the sea would go on into infinity.' Lizzie hugged him back.

He kissed her as the crowds milled around them. She pulled away.

'What's wrong?'

'Everyone's watching.'

'This is New York. Nobody gives a damn about anyone else. And I certainly couldn't care less.' He kissed her again. 'What kept you away from me for so long?' he murmured into her ear.

'Circumstances.'

'Give me your suitcases. Let's go.'

She moved away from him, silent, watching him. His hair was cut in the new crewcut style, and lightened by the sun. He caught her eye.

'Do I come up to standard?'

'You look—' she wanted to say 'gorgeous', but the uncertainty she always felt in his presence prevented her.

'What?'

'Great.' She looked away.

He took her hand and pulled her towards him. 'You look great yourself.'

She blushed.

As they walked into the car park, the warm wind blew around them, amplifying the noise of the traffic, the cry of the gulls, the bustle of activity around the ship as it unloaded its cargo. He kept his hand in hers and led her through the rows of cars.

'You sure know your way around.'

'If you don't pick things up here pretty smartly, you get left behind.'

The wind blew warm in her face. 'Lovely,' she sighed.

'Yeh, and New York is murder. We'll go upstate. I know the place. Do some fishing, go swimming—'

'Remember the long summer evenings down the seafront, when you bought your first car?'

He smiled. 'This is my new one.' He stood before a four-door sedan. 'Like it?'

'It's beautiful,' she said, eyeing the chrome gleaming in the sun, her surprise evident in her face.

He opened the passenger door and removed his jacket, folding it and placing it on the back seat, before holding the door for Lizzie and then walking around the car and slipping into the driver's seat.

'It's so comfortable.' She sank into the soft leather.

'It's brand new on the market.' With a smile of satisfaction, he turned on the ignition.

'You've done well.'

'I want to do better.'

'I worried about you so much when you first left home.'

'Good.'

He steered the car out into the snarling traffic.

'I've never seen so many cars.'

'You'll get used to it. Everyone's rushing, which makes life a bit frightening at first. I still hate the subways.' He made a face. 'It's too hot to breathe in them.'

They drove in silence. Lizzie watched with amazement as the tall buildings fell back around City Hall, and Central Park. Across Brooklyn Bridge, past the Municipal Building, she looked down over the river, at the sailboats tugging against the ebbing tide.

'It's beautiful,' she said.

'It sure is.'

Pete's apartment was in a seven-storeyed brown building with no architectural distinction. He followed Lizzie inside, pressed a buzzer and a lift rumbled above. It took them to the sixth floor. A door marked 'P. Scanlon' opened into a long room, furnished with a couch and an assortment of chairs. A screen divided it from his bedroom, which comprised a large bed and a television set encased in a cabinet. The tiny kitchen and bathroom were sectioned off by plasterboard. The whole place had a clean, uncluttered look.

'It's what's known as a studio apartment.'

Lizzie sat down on the couch. 'Very comfortable,' she said, looking around approvingly.

He hung up his jacket. 'Let me get you a drink.'

He went into the kitchen and returned with a bottle of champagne and two glasses.

'Here's to us.' He handed her a glass of champagne.

Pete suddenly looked shy. 'In case you're worried, I've booked you a room in the hotel around the corner.'

'That's kind of you. Thank you.'

He sat down beside her. 'Would your mother approve?'

'Definitely.'

There was a fleeting look of bitterness in his face. 'Nothing I ever did was good enough for her.'

'To be fair to her, Pete, she was worried about your gambling.'

'She needn't have. I told you I'd give it up, and I did.' He looked at her. 'Were you worried?'

'You did go a bit mad on the horses for a while.'

'Only to help me scrape by. I was hard-up, Lizzie. Not any more. With my salary, I have enough to live on. I'm earning $5,000 a year now.'

'I'm impressed.'

'Good.'

They ate in an Italian restaurant nearby, and later Pete carried her bags as they walked to the hotel.

'Tomorrow I'll show you some of the sights, and guess what? I've got tickets for *Kiss Me Kate* at the New Century Theatre. You like Cole Porter?'

He danced Lizzie around the street, signing snippets from '*I Hate Men*' and '*Always True to You in my Fashion*'.

'Wonderful, wonderful!' Lizzie collapsed against him laughing. 'Where are we off to then?'

He put his finger to her lips. 'No questions. It's a surprise. Now I had better go and let you get some sleep. We have a busy time ahead of us.'

They drove fast; the landscape flashed by, under a blue sky. His driving became demonic as he over took car after car. The road signs pointed to Connecticut.

'We might as well have our picnic while it's still sunny.' He drove down a narrow track.

Pete stopped the car, and took the picnic basket and a rug from the boot. They walked among the birch trees, past a rushing stream, across a plank bridge. The ground was littered with colourful leaves which rustled as they walked through them. They spread out the rug under one of the trees. From a basket laden with food he took bread, cheese, ham, tomatoes, hard-boiled eggs, and proceeded to lay them on a cloth.

'Red or white wine?' he asked.

'You've thought of everything.'

'Except the salt.'

Later, while the sun was at its hottest, they stretched

out to rest. Pete held her hand. 'It's good to have you with me.'

'I think I'm dreaming, that I'll wake up and find myself in my little bed in the nurses' home.'

'This is no dream, and we still have our holiday ahead of us.'

They lay in each other's arms. Lizzie dozed off. When the sun began to slide westwards, and the wind rose, Pete nudged her awake. 'Time to go, sleepy head.'

They stopped at a whitewashed farmhouse, and were welcomed into its cool, flagged hallway by an Indian woman. She led them to the kitchen, where saucepans bubbled on the stove, and a scrubbed table was set for two. The smell of meat roasting in the oven, mingled with herbs and spices, permeated the room.

'You like?' The Indian woman's brown eyes glittered.

'I like,' Lizzie assured her.

'Ready soon. Glass of wine?'

Pete opened a door onto a patio. 'Come and see the view.'

Flowers tumbled from terracotta pots and spilled over into flowerbeds. Hens pecked at the ground in a leisurely way, and the breeze stirred. Although she was thousands of miles from home, there was a comforting familiarity about the place. It reminded Lizzie of her Uncle Mike's farm, and she was filled with a sense of *déjà vu*. She turned and watched Pete pouring the wine, relaxed and happy. He handed her a glass.

'To us,' he said.

'To this beautiful house. It's not your first time here.'

'I've been here a couple of times before.'

'That's why you are so at ease.'

'I love it. The greenery reminds me of home, and it's the nearest place to get away from the frantic pace of New York.'

She picked up the courage to ask: 'Who with?'

'Some blonde or other. Can't remember.'

She gazed at him, unsure of his implication.

'Hey.' He came to her, taking her in his arms. 'Lizzie, you've got tears in your eyes. I didn't mean to upset you. I'm not a saint. There have been one or two women. But I've never been serious about them or brought them here. I come up here alone to relax. It's taken me a long time to get this far. I've worked hard to make something for myself, to have something to share with whomever I settle down with. You'll never know how much I envied you and Vicky having a home with two reliable parents there to look after you, and a gran thrown in for good measure. All I had was a sick mother and a drunken father. That's why I don't want to get married until I have something solid in my life.' He lowered his voice. 'Security for my wife and children.'

'You're thinking very far ahead.'

'Am I?' He looked uncomfortable. 'Don't forget, Lizzie, my father was a wretched man, burdened with money problems. We used to wish he'd take off to the war and,

God forgive me for saying it, never come back, even if only to give my mother a bit of peace.'

'He wasn't all bad.'

'No. He worked for Mrs de Winter. Did her garden and odd jobs around the place. You remember the de Winters?'

'Yes. They were back from India. She wore a hat with a wide brim, and dresses down to her ankles. I remember she would call, "Afternoon tea on the lawn", to my mother, and produce a beautifully laid tray with cucumber sandwiches. Gran called them "Protestant sandwiches". They were wafer thin and she said they hadn't a bite in them.'

'The de Winters were good employers; used to servants. Mrs de Winter sometimes sent food home to my mother, a cooked chicken, jellied eels, figs in aspic. What we wouldn't eat my mother took to Mrs Tomkins, the woman she worked for. One day my father stole Mr de Winter's gold fob watch, and pawned it. He meant to redeem it and give it back, but he spent the money on drink. He was fired. Life became intolerable, with my mother working all day, and giving him money to keep him out of the way.' Pete's face was contorted with the pain of remembering. 'I should have stayed and helped her. That's my biggest regret. It was only when she died that I realised how miserable her life had been. Stuck in a basement all her married life, and her health so delicate.'

'You came home to her.'

'Yes. Crippled and penniless from the war.'

'You had your pension.'

'I came home to you too.'

'I didn't realise that.'

'It was difficult to face the problems of my childhood then. I took refuge in forgetfulness. To admit I loved people as flawed as my parents was a sign of weakness as far as I was concerned. To admit I loved anyone, even you, was a sign of weakness. I took it for granted that you knew. We went everywhere together that summer I bought the car.'

'You were recuperating from your war injuries. It wasn't easy to read your mind. Just when I'd think that everything was wonderful between us, you would become distant, or disappear. I never knew where I stood with you.'

Pete looked away. 'I suppose I was afraid to get too involved because I had nothing. Then the day of May Tully's wedding I realised I wasn't wanted by your family. The look on your mother's face said, "My daughter has a career and a future, and you're not going to interfere with it." She was looking down her nose at me.'

'No she wasn't. She didn't want me to get serious about anyone because of what she had gone through with Karen.'

'Whatever her reasons, I was determined to make something of myself.' He raised his glass. 'To Gertie, for giving me the shove I needed to better myself.'

Suddenly Lizzie realised how much she had missed Pete's teasing insults. The compulsion in him to better himself had taken him across the world away from her, when they should have been together. An understanding began to grow between them, as they recognised how lonely they had been for one another.

'Do you think you'll be happy here with me?' Pete looked anxious.

'I think I'll be very happy.'

'I'll take good care of you.'

'I know.'

'Let's have dinner.'

Afterwards they unpacked and settled in, Lizzie in her room, Pete in his.

Later, they explored the house so Lizzie could get her bearings, then went outside across the stone-flagged patio, past outhouses and storerooms, until they came to the stables. A horse whinnied behind one of the doors.

'We'll go fishing tomorrow.' Pete examined the boat in the yard. 'I'll have a look at the engine, and get some oilskins from Tom.'

'Who is Tom?'

'Anna, the Indian woman's husband. He's the local farmer, and caretaker. He taught me to fish.'

It was a quiet house, full of secrets. Gradually it seduced them into its leisurely pace. Pete fixed the outboard engine of the boat and they went fishing on the lake.

Other days they swam, sunbathing on the jetty afterwards. They danced in the evenings on the patio to the singing of Peggy Lee, and watched the sun make its westward descent. Sometimes they waited to see the moon etched on the eastern horizon, always listening to the cicadas. Anna brought their food, and cooked their evening meal. Her movements were so quiet that the delicious smell of cooking was usually the only indication of her presence.

The intense heat gave way to torrential rain. They stayed indoors, listened to music and talked. One evening Pete made a log fire, and put a Peggy Lee and Dave Barbour record on the gramophone. Lizzie was curled up by the fire, leafing through a magazine, when Pete suddenly said, 'Lizzie, will you marry me?'

Her magazine fell to the floor.

'What did you say?'

'I asked you to marry me. I'm doing well in business. I don't gamble any more. Not even a flutter as your gran would say. You don't have to give me an answer straight away.' He stood up and went to the window. 'It's stopped raining. Would you like to go for a walk?'

She went to him, put her arms around his neck, and began to cry.

He held her tight. 'I didn't expect a reaction like this . . .'

'Take no notice. I'm happy.'

'I'd hate to see you when you're sad.'

They both laughed.

'I'd love to marry you,' Lizzie told him. 'It's what I've always wanted.'

'I'll make you happy, I promise.'

'I know you will.'

'We'll celebrate. I'll phone the restaurant and order champagne.'

'Wait, Pete. I'd like to tell Mam and Dad before we do anything.'

'Are you sure – what if they try and stop you?'

'If Mam couldn't talk me out of coming here, she's not going to try to stop me from marrying you.'

Pete looked uncertain. 'If you're sure. I love you, Lizzie. I've never said that to any other girl.'

'What about Vicky?'

'Especially not Vicky.'

They laughed.

'How do you feel now?' Pete asked.

'Overjoyed.' Lizzie hugged him.

Lizzie placed a long-distance call to Ireland. When the tinny voice of the international operator finally phoned back to say that she had made the connection, and that Mr Doyle was on the line, Lizzie's heart flipped.

'Dad, it's Lizzie.'

'Lizzie! Is everything all right?' His voice was faint.

'Everything's wonderful. Pete and I are engaged.'

'Very good. Here's your mother.'

'We were expecting it.' Gertie's voice was clear and matter-of-fact.

'Are you pleased?'

'You're sensible enough to know what you want.'

'It's all I ever wanted, Mam.'

'I know and I'm happy for you.'

12

Gran stood looking at her reflection in the mirror, wrinkling her nose disdainfully at her new woollen frock. She touched her crinkled skin, as she studied the pouches behind her glasses, her withered mouth, the loose flesh around her chin. Why had she not noticed these things before? Sissy will see the changes in me, she thought. Well, I'm getting old. So was Sissy though. That thought gave her a little satisfaction. She wondered about Sissy. Would she be fat? Was her hair grey? Hardly. Sissy was such a glamour puss.

The burgundy frock Gertie had bought her in Clery's was plain, she decided. Looking around her cluttered dressing table, she found her jewellery box and rummaged through it, until she unearthed her diamond and ruby broach. She tidied her hair into a net, and took one last look in the mirror, before going downstairs to welcome home the daughter she had not seen for twenty years.

Gertie was busy in the kitchen, basting the crackling of the roast of pork Bob Quinn had delivered that morning.

'I want to get the potatoes nice and crispy,' she said as Gran came into the kitchen.

'How do I look?'

'That dress is perfect on you.'

'Perfect me foot. How could anythin' be perfect on me? Look at me, mouth droolin', eyes half-closed. I'm gettin' old, Gertie, and worse still, I'm shrinkin'.'

Gertie laughed. 'I never knew you to be so anxious about your appearance before.'

'Hm. Sissy'll be eyein' me up and down.'

'She'll be so delighted to see you, she won't notice the changes.'

Gertie was thinking how lucky Sissy was that Gran was alive. That time she got pneumonia, and almost died, Sissy was too busy fighting a war to write to her. Several times, when Gertie urged her to come home to see her mother, her letters were ignored. Who would have thought that robust, fun-loving Sissy would be coming home to convalesce?

Tying on an apron to protect her dress, Gran began drying the dishes.

Gertie took the tea towel from her hand. 'You don't want to tire yourself out before they arrive.'

'Then I'll bring in the washin'. It was a good dryin' day. By the way, where's John?'

'Down with the Quinns. He went to ask what day Patsy's coming home.'

'He's obsessed with that child.'

'I'm afraid to let him out of my sight since he ran off to Newcastle.'

'Will I ever forget the fright he gave us.'

'You knew nothing about it until it was all over.'

'It was still a shock. Think of what might have happened to the poor little mite.'

'I think he learned his lesson. The Sergeant in Bray said he was terrified when they picked him up.'

'He won't run off in a hurry again. Anyway, Patsy's coming home now, so he should settle down.'

'She's made a miraculous recovery.'

'She's not out of the woods yet.. They're only letting her home for a week to see how she copes.'

'Better keep John away from her for another while.'

'That's going to be difficult. He can't wait to see her, and who could blame him? Don't bother with the washing. They'll be here any minute.'

Gran ignored her. Taking her stick, she went out across the garden to remove the washing from the clothes line, which ran almost the length of the garden. Birds sang and a light breeze rustled the trees as she slowly removed shirts, socks and nightdresses. As she moved along, she was so filled with delight at the prospect of seeing Vicky again that she forgot all about Sissy. She looked around the garden – at the roses, lupins and hollyhocks, their blooms faded. The last of the daisies dotted through the grass reminded her of Vicky and Lizzie sitting there, endlessly threading them to make daisy chains. She looked at the vegetable patch, and thanked God for giving Bill the strength to dig and weed and plant, and for the apple trees that yielded enough fruit for the tarts she and Gertie had baked. Everyone loved her apple tarts. Gran was grateful to God for sparing her to see her beloved grandchildren growing up, and for curing Patsy.

Remembering the time Bill had brought her up from Limerick, she realised that she had intended to return home after a week. She had held on to her cottage for a year, refusing to sell it in case she wanted to go back. Bill finally had persuaded her to sell it when her health was at a low ebb.

When she became ill soon after, and had to go to hospital, they had administered the last sacraments. She thought she was going to die. It was only then that she made up her mind to stay with Bill and Gertie. One of the advantages of old age, she decided, was that people expected less of her, and she had more time. Time was not so important any more. What little she had left was too precious to waste on worrying about the future. So she spent it remembering the past.

All her life she had been in a hurry because of her responsibilities to other people. First her parents, then her children. Cooking, cleaning, getting them to school, worrying about how she would provide for them when her husband had died suddenly. She would be concerned about them until she died.

Gran was a religious woman who gratefully accepted God's will. It was clear now that it had been God's will that she would not have to live alone. Bill and Gertie's family had given her a new lease on life.

That's how Vicky found her, leaning against the garden shed, the washing in a pile on the grass.

'Gran, what are you standing there for? Are you all right?'

She turned slowly, saw her, and opened her arms to a joyful Vicky.

'Oh Gran!' Vicky finally released her, her voice choked with tears. 'It's wonderful to see you. Darling, darling Gran.'

Gran said, 'Cut out the nonsense, Vicky, and let me look at you.' Astounded, she said, 'Don't tell me you're wearin' trousers.' Her eyes were on Vicky's tailored slacks and suede jacket.

Vicky did a twirl. 'All the rage in Canada.'

'I'm not impressed. If God wanted you to look like that, you'd have been born a man.'

'Changing fashion, Gran. Have to go with the times. Come and see Mother.'

Sissy was standing at the back door, waiting.

'Is it yourself, Sissy?' Gran straightened up. 'I wouldn't have known you.'

Sissy came forward and gave her mother a peck on the cheek. 'How are you, Mother?' she said stiffly.

If her mother's appearance surprised her, it did not show in her face.

'As you see me – old.'

Vicky put down the washing, her eyes warily watching.

'I brought you something,' Sissy said.

Gran painfully lowered herself into a chair and said, 'You needn't have bothered. What is it?'

'I'll get it. Won't be a minute.'

'She looks well. Bit on the plump side, but well,' Gran said to Gertie when Sissy had left the room.

'Heart patients can be very deceptive,' Vicky said. 'There are no external scars, so you have to watch for signs.'

'What signs?' Instinctively, Gran put her hand on her chest.

'Little things like shortness of breath, pains in the arms, tightening across the chest.'

'I've pains everywhere.' Gran rubbed her arms.

Sissy returned with a bottle of brandy.

'This should do you good, Mother.' She put it down on the table.

'Well that's kind of you. I'll have a drop now I think.'

'Before your dinner?' Gertie was surprised.

'Just a taste of it. I feel a flutterin' in me chest.'

Gertie put glasses on the table and poured a tot into each glass.

'Here's to you, Sissy. It's wonderful to have you home.' She handed Sissy a glass.

Gran raised her glass. 'It's good to see you. Don't have another heart attack while you're here.'

'Mother.' Gertie threw her a scornful look.

'She's a bit pale.'

'I'm fine.'

Gran sipped her drink. The brandy warmed her. 'You're more subdued than I remember. Of course, old age is a terrible thing,' she sighed, the colour rising in her cheeks.

'I'm not old,' Sissy protested.

'You're not young either. Tell me, Sissy, what exactly happened to you?'

Sissy glared at her mother. 'There's not much to tell. I must have blacked out. Luckily Myrtle was staying with me and called an ambulance.'

'You should have stayed married to Hermy. He's better than nothin' at all.'

'I am married to Hermy.'

'It isn't a proper marriage, with him in one country, and you in another.'

'I'm going to unpack. Coming, Gran?' Vicky asked.

'Might as well.' Gran drained her glass and, leaning on Vicky's arm, left the room.

'Take no notice of her if she's a bit cranky. It's her age,' Gertie said when Gran had gone.

'I don't remember her any different and I've known her a lot longer than you have.'

'She hasn't been well lately, though she won't admit it.'

'How do you put up with her and her caustic remarks? You're a saint.'

'Not at all. She's a wonderful woman, and a tower of strength to me.'

'How is Karen?'

'Coming home tomorrow with Hank. We'll have a full house again, thank God. They've been gone six months now.'

'Good. That'll keep mother out of my hair. By the way, Gertie, just because I had a heart attack doesn't mean I'm an invalid. I'll help with the chores.'

'I'm relying on you.'

'Shall I call John? I can't wait to see him.'

'Yes. He'll want to meet you too.'

The wind blew across the sea, lifting and separating the waves. As the clouds gathered, the mail boat came into view, moving forward slowly, heaving as it wrestled with the tide. John, standing with Gertie, shivered with the cold and the excitement of seeing his mother again. The thought of facing Hank filled him with dread.

'Thank God they're safe,' Gertie said as she saw the boat. 'It's over an hour late.'

John watched them coming down the gangplank. Hank, head bent, holding his wind-battered hat with his hand. Karen, scuttling for shelter, ran straight into her mother's arms.

'Mam!'

Gertie held her as she would a frightened child and said, 'I thought you'd never get here'.

Karen hugged John. In her arms he felt safe. When she released him, he noticed how pale her face was, in spite of the lipstick and powder she was wearing.

'Hello, Hank.' Gertie shook hands with him. 'What a terrible evening. Was it a dreadful crossing?'

'Pretty rough.' Hank's smile was as chilly as the air around them. 'Where's Bill?'

'Waiting in the car.'

He took Karen's arm and drew her forward, away from John, whom he ignored. Gertie followed, John trailing after her.

'Dreadful night.' Bill took the suitcases and put them in the boot.

'Sit with me, darling.' Karen pulled John into the back seat beside her. 'How are you?'

'All right.'

'Is that all?'

'I thought you were never coming home. Auntie Sissy's here with Vicky.'

'I'm dying to meet them.'

The burst of excitement that followed Karen's reunion with Sissy and Vicky was too much for Hank. He went into the kitchen and poured himself a brandy, shutting the door behind him.

'He's a dish.' Vicky looked admiringly in the direction of the kitchen.

'Not a very sociable one,' Gertie snapped.

'The crossing was rough. I was sick all the way over.' Karen looked miserable.

'The waves were monstrous. No wonder you were sick,' Gertie said.

'The whole sea was like a tiger, wasn't it darling?' Karen said to John.

'It was like a great angry lion.'

'Isn't it time he was in bed?' Hank glared at John when they all filed into the kitchen for supper.

John looked defiant. 'I'm allowed to stay up late tonight.'

'Of course you are, lovey,' Gertie said. 'You see little enough of your mother.'

'I'm going to take a bath,' Hank said to Karen. 'I'll have a bit of privacy there.' He put down his glass and left the room.

'What's up with him?' Bill asked Karen.

She sighed. 'He's fed up because everything went against him in his business deals.'

'He certainly took his time getting things done. We were expecting you home months ago.'

John put his arms around Karen.

'Don't take any notice.' Gertie looked concerned.

'After supper, I'll read you a story,' Vicky told John.

'Great.' John looked hopefully at Karen. 'You could come and hear it, Mom.'

'Maybe Hank would like to hear it?' Vicky said.

'Hank doesn't listen to stories. He doesn't have time.'

'Perhaps I could persuade him. It might improve his temper.' Vicky winked at John. 'I'll go and ask him.'

'He's in the bath,' Karen said. 'He takes a long time.'

Vicky smiled at her. 'Time is one thing I have plenty of. I'll wait for him.'

Karen turned away.

Later, when Gertie had Karen to herself, she said, 'There's something up between you and Hank, isn't there?'

Karen's eyes met hers. 'It's just that everything seems to be going wrong for him. The people he makes appointments to see either don't show up, or refuse to do business with him. Now he wants to go back to the States.'

'Well, it's his home. You can't blame him for that.'

'I know. The trouble is he doesn't want to take John.'

Gertie made no attempt to conceal her astonishment. 'And what does he propose you do with John? Leave him here with us? Of course, we'd be delighted to—'

'Nothing as simple as that. He wants to send him to boarding school.'

'Boarding school – the idea of it!'

'I know. That's what the rows were about. He won't listen to me. Says I know nothing about rearing children and that John is spoilt. I suppose the fact that the child ran away from home has a lot to do with it.'

'It's more likely that he wants to get him out of the way.'

'Boarding school didn't do Vicky and Lizzie any harm, did it?'

'They were twelve and thirteen years of age at the time, Karen.' Gertie lowered her voice. 'Vicky was an evacuee and there was a war on. She needed a bit of discipline, not to mention a decent education. Besides, she was a devil for the boys, and a bad influence on Lizzie.'

'Judging by the way she's behaving with Hank, she hasn't changed much. She is very beautiful.'

'Yes she is, and she knows it. But the situation with John is totally different. It's pathetic the way he has been thrown from Billy to Jack. The child is lonely. He missed you, Karen. After all, he had you to himself in North Carolina.'

'I missed him too, and I regretted every minute I was away from him. But I don't want to lose Hank. Oh God, why does everything have to be so complicated.'

'Life is never simple. It strikes me that Hank doesn't want to share you with John and that's your problem. You may yet have to make a choice between them.'

There was silence. 'And if that's the case,' Gertie continued, 'John should be your obvious choice.'

Her words fell like blows on Karen's ears. She looked at her mother.

'I don't know what to do. Would it be so bad to put John in boarding school until we sort something out?'

Gertie began clearing the table. 'It's your decision, of

course. There's one thing that must be said in all this. You, Karen, are a very selfish girl.'

'What?'

'You heard what I said. You seem to be interested in pleasing yourself, before you take anyone else into consideration. Right back to the time you went off to England to nurse. You insisted on going over there. Met Paul, got pregnant, married Paul, went back to England. You hardly had any time with him before he was sent off on his secret missions. You had John, and Paul went missing. I don't want to rake up unhappy memories, but did you once consult us about any of it? Look at you now with Hank. Is he suitable? Are you happy? Racing around after him instead of sitting down to plan your future, and the future of that precious child of yours.' Gertie took a breath. 'He should be the most important person in your life. Oh, what's the use?' Exhausted, she sat down.

Karen got to her feet. 'I'm sorry to have upset you, Mam. I suppose I'm a bit inconsiderate where you and Dad are concerned.'

'That's putting it mildly.' Gertie pursed her lips to prevent herself from saying anything else.

Karen began to wash the dishes, but Gertie stopped her. 'Leave those. I'll do them. Go and say goodnight to John, and try and calm Hank down a bit.'

Karen looked as if she was about to say something, then suddenly seemed lost for words. 'Goodnight, Mam.'

She gave her mother a kiss on the cheek. 'I love you.'

When she had left the room, Gertie slowly did the washing up and tidied the kitchen. She heard John's high-pitched laughter coming from upstairs, Hank calling out to Karen to stop the noise. Gertie hoped that Hank would not cause her as much heartbreak as Paul's disappearance had done. She put out the milk bottles, locked the front door, and went upstairs. Bill was in bed, reading.

She sat on the edge of the bed. 'Hank wants Karen to send John to boarding school.'

Bill put down the paper. 'What?'

'I gave her a piece of my mind. I think I went too far.' Suddenly she was in tears.

'What did you say?'

Gertie wiped her hand across her eyes. 'I said what I've been thinking for a long time. That she's a selfish girl and always has been.'

'What was her reaction to that?'

'She didn't want to listen.'

'Typical. When Karen has problems, she keeps her feelings to herself, as if there's nothing wrong.'

'She wouldn't have said anything only she's worried about John. I hope I didn't go too far, that's all.'

'If you felt you had to speak up, then you were right to do so. Hank seemed all right to me when he came here first. Now I'm not so sure.'

'What do you mean?'

'He's a peculiar genius. Sharp with Karen and intolerant with John. I'm worried too.'

Gertie dried her eyes. 'That's something at least. You usually think I'm over-reacting.'

'Gertie, have a bit of sense. Have I ever questioned your judgment?'

'Where Karen is concerned, I don't often have your support.'

'Look. I'm not happy about Hank. But that's beside the point. She obviously likes him and we can't interfere.'

'Surely we have some say where John's concerned.'

'He's her son. I'll talk to her tomorrow.'

'She seems so alone sometimes.'

'She has a dread of being on her own.'

'She has no friends.'

'Doesn't stay anywhere long enough to make friends.'

Gertie considered this. 'I don't understand it. If she'd had a terrible childhood, with no parents to depend on, I could make allowances.'

'You're a wonderful mother, Gertie. She knows that. But Paul's disappearance was a terrible thing to happen to her. We can't expect her to behave like an ordinary person after that. Her life was shattered.'

'All she ever wanted was to be married to Paul, with a home of her own.'

'She's lonely all right. I was too hard on her. It's the responsibility of it all.' Gertie began to weep.

'You're tired. Come to bed and don't worry.'

She lay in bed for a long time after Bill had gone to sleep, gazing into the darkness, glad of his support, but terrified of the future. She realised as she began to relax that it was fear that was making her abrasive.

13

It was early September and there was a nip in the air in the mornings.

'Why do I have to go to boarding school?' John persisted when Karen told him they were going to Dublin to buy his uniform.

'Because it's a good idea.'

'But why are you sending me away?'

'We haven't got a proper home for you yet. There are too many distractions here. In boarding school you'll have the security we can't give you. And you can't run away. Anyway Hank thinks—'

'I'm sick of what he thinks.'

John suddenly saw Hank standing in the doorway. 'That's enough. No more discussion, Karen. He'll do as he's told.' He shut the door firmly on them.

'You heard him.' Karen's voice was quivering.

'I hate him,' John glowered.

'Don't say that, darling. You know it upsets me. Tell you what: if you're very good and don't make a fuss, I'll take you away for a little holiday before school begins.'

'Hank won't like that.'

'Mrs Keogh's niece has a cottage to rent in a fishing village in Wexford. We could spend a few days on our own there. Would you like that?'

'Yippee! Can Patsy come too?'

Karen hesitated, then seeing the expression of hope on John's face, said, 'I don't see why not. I'll talk to her mother, but I don't know if she'll let her miss any more school. She's missed a lot already.'

'Mrs Quinn won't mind if she thinks it would do Patsy good.' Later, John explained to his father privately about his dread of boarding school. How he was afraid that the other boys would not talk to him, and how much he would miss his mother. Something he was reluctant to admit aloud.

Mrs Quinn agreed that a few days at the seaside would do Patsy all the good in the world. John wanted to tell her but Karen asked him to keep it secret for a while.

Hank did not appear again that evening, to John's great relief. Later, when he heard Karen telling Gertie that Hank would be going to Galway for a few days to attend a conference on forestry, he was overjoyed. He had managed to see Patsy every day since she had come home from the sanatorium. Because she was not allowed out, she began to teach him poems from her favourite books. She would write them down in her copybook, so that he could learn them when he was on his own. She urged him to practise his writing too.

'Write to me often. Then you won't feel so lonely.'

Next morning he went to see her as soon as Gertie had gone to mass. Patsy was sitting by the fire reading *Little Women*. 'Anthony told me you were off to Dublin to get new clothes.'

'A uniform.'

'Aren't you delighted?'

He made a face.

'When I get a new pair of shoes,' Pasty said, I think I'm in heaven, especially now that I know I'll get the wear out of them.'

'You'll wear out lots of pairs of shoes.'

She had put on weight and her skin glowed. 'I don't cough any more,' she said proudly. 'Soon I won't have to go back to Newcastle for my check-ups. I'll be able to have them in the clinic.'

'You won't be sorry about that.'

'I'll miss Nurse Dillon. She was good to me. Aren't you excited about going to boarding school?'

'How can anyone get excited about anything to do with boarding school?'

'You'll get to love it. Midnight feasts, a tuck shop. I was reading all about boarding school in that magazine, *School Girl's Own Library*.'

'I won't love it. I'll hate it. They think I won't run away, but I will.'

'What would you do a stupid thing like that for?'

'So that I wouldn't have to go back.'

'That's childish.'

'It's all right for you – you don't have to go.'

'I wish I could.'

'When is the christening?' John asked to change the subject.

'Sunday. Mammy's coming home from hospital on Friday. I'm dying to see the new baby.'

'Haven't you seen him yet?'

'No. I have to mind the house while Daddy goes to the hospital. It's only for a few days.'

'I know a secret,' John said suddenly.

'What?'

'Can't tell. It's a secret.'

Patsy looked annoyed. 'Why did you say anything in the first place?'

'Because you're supposed to beg me to tell you.'

'Well I won't. Keep it to yourself and see if I care.'

The salesman measured John for his school blazer and trousers. Karen ticked off her list as he added a cap, two shirts, a tie, socks, underwear, and winter vests.

'You look like a proper gentleman,' he said, straightening John's tie.

Karen stood back to admire him. 'What do you think?'

'Horrible.' John's eyes were on the crest of the outsized blazer. 'Anthony will have a good laugh when he sees me dressed up like this.'

Later that evening Gran sat in front of Lizzie's old

school trunk, sewing on name tapes until her eyes were closing in her head.

John went upstairs and slammed his bedroom door.

'Has he been misbehaving?' Hank asked Karen when he came in.

'He's been as good as gold.'

Bob Quinn came up from the basement and knocked on the door. 'Here you are, Mrs D,' he said to Gertie. 'A lovely bit of stewing steak.'

'Thanks, Bob. Sure you always have the best of everything.'

'Mary Carney didn't think that this morning.'

'Why?'

'She came in for a chicken and I showed her the only one we had. She took one look at it and said, "Are you joking me, Bob? Call that scrawny thing a chicken? You must have something better than that. Only Father O'Brien's having dinner guests." '

' "Dinner guests", if you don't mind,' said Gertie.

'I went out the back with the chicken, took the pump off the bike and pumped up it up a bit, stuck a skewer in it, and took it out to her. "Oh, that's a better one," she said. Then just as I was wrapping it up, she said, "Do you know what, Bob, I think I'll take the other one with it." '

Gertie roared laughing. 'What did you do?' she asked.

'What could I do? I had to sneak out the back door and run up the road to buy one.'

'You're a terrible man, Bob Quinn. A terrible man.' Gertie was still laughing when he left.

'He makes it up half the time,' Gran said when Gertie told her. 'More in his line to come home in time for his tea.'

'Do you think that Hank hates children and that's why he's sending me away?' John asked Anthony the next day.

They were all in the coach house – Biddy and Annie Plunkett, Patsy, Rasher and Banger. Anthony had won the National Junior Boxing Championships the week before, and Bill and Gertie were giving them a little party to celebrate.

'I dunno. Could be. He's a queer fish anyway.'

John looked at Biddy. 'Maybe neither of them likes me?'

'Don't be stupid. Your mother loves you, you know that. She might be a bit afraid of him though.' Biddy was painting her nails blood red. 'Do you like this colour, Anthony?'

Anthony looked at his watch. 'What's keeping Spud? He's in charge of the music.' He moved around restlessly.

'My mother's not afraid of anyone,' John persisted.

Biddy sighed. 'I don't mean "afraid" that way. I mean afraid he might leave her if she doesn't go along with his wishes.'

'I wish he would leave her.'

'That's the difference. She doesn't,' Anthony said.

'How do you know?' John asked.

Biddy cast Anthony a loving look. 'Anthony's very wise in the ways of the world.'

Anthony ignored her. 'It's simple,' he said. 'If she didn't want him, she'd get rid of him.'

'Mightn't be that simple. You'd have a job getting rid of me,' Biddy said.

Anthony looked at her. 'Who says I want to? If I did, I would. Make no mistake about that.'

'Don't put a damper on things,' Biddy said to John. 'Let's enjoy ourselves.'

Bill came up the stairs carrying a heavy cardboard box, Mrs Keogh following with another one.

'You're earlier than we thought,' he panted. 'Give us a hand there, Anthony.'

Anthony helped them unload plates of sandwiches, cakes, biscuits, jelly and trifle onto a makeshift wooden bench.

Standing, hands clasped behind his back, Bill Doyle surveyed the scene. 'You've done a wonderful job with the decorations.'

Fairy lights dotted the ceiling, paper-chains made from crepe paper and cut in the shape of boxing gloves were strewn around the walls, streamers hung here and there.

'Biddy did most of it,' Anthony said.

'Clever girl.'

Biddy took a bow in her new scarlet dress, revealing more of her young breasts than Mrs Keogh deemed modest. 'Brazen hussy,' she muttered as she vigorously polished the knives with a paper serviette before laying them out on the table.

'Tuck in everyone,' Bill said. 'You're growing children. There's a crate of lemonade in the house, Anthony. Will you come and get it?'

'That's very kind of you, Mr Doyle,'

'Compliments of the Home and Colonial. Don't you deserve it? Our champion and we're proud of you.'

Anthony's eyes shone as he said with a smirk, 'This is only the start. Some day I aim to knock Joe Lewis out in the first round.'

Spud came dashing up the stairs to announce that Anthony had been picked for the County Dublin team to play in a tournament in London, in a month's time. A burst of *For He's a Jolly Good Fellow* followed. Anthony's face reddened. He raised his clenched fists in the air.

Mrs Keogh shook his hand. 'Well done, Anthony,' she exclaimed. 'I never thought you'd make anything of yourself. And look at Spud here, not far behind you.'

Once Spud and Anthony had made up their differences, Spud signed up for boxing lessons at the Workmen's Club with Mr Murphy.

Spud looked proud. 'Best thing I ever did was join the boxing. Only for you, I wouldn't have thought of it.'

'Only for me da, I'd never have thought if it either.'

'If you hadn't nearly killed Spud that time, no one would have thought of it,' Mrs Keogh added.

'Here's to me da,' laughed Anthony. 'You never know, I might become a professional boxer yet. Wait, I have to get the minerals before we can have a toast.'

'There are no professional boxers in Ireland,' Spud said.

'Then I'll have to go and live in England, won't I?'

Biddy's face fell.

'I'll leave you to it, but no boisterous behaviour, mind,' Bill said. 'Mrs Doyle will be over later with more food.'

'Thanks, Mr Doyle,' they yelled and, laughing and talking, they began to eat. Spud played *Candy Kisses Wrapped in Paper* on his gramophone and Anthony and Biddy danced.

'Taking anyone to London with you?' she said, snuggling up to him.

'I might.'

Biddy said, 'I love you.'

John heard her and was so impressed that he temporarily forgot how miserable he was.

Someone put on Bob Hope singing *Buttons and Bows*, and Biddy hummed along.

Mrs Quinn came into the room, the new baby in her arms. 'What a racket. You'll waken the dead.' But her eyes immediately fell on the sagging floorboards. 'Take it easy, or you'll find yourselves downstairs quicker than you expected.'

★   ★   ★

Two days later, Karen took Patsy and John by train to Wexford. Mrs Keogh's niece, Nancy, and her husband met them at the station in Ballyragget, and drove them to Nancy's cottage. That afternoon she loaned them bicycles and they cycled slowly past fields and hedgerows, up a hill toward the ocean. When the hill got too steep, they wheeled their bicycles. Below them was the vast expanse of sea, blue and sparkling in the sun.

'Wow,' John shouted with delight.

Patsy leaned her bicycle against a wall and sat in a ditch to get her breath back. When she had recovered, they walked their bicycles down the hill and cycled into the fishing village. The streets were narrow and they eased their way along cobblestones, past a pub, and a fish and chip shop. The strong smell of chips made their mouths water. Down at the harbour they stood gazing at the fishing boats. All John's worries about going to boarding school in a few days drifted away as they sat in the sunshine watching groups of fishermen untangling their nets, their laughter carrying on the wind. Further out, sailboats bobbed, and a light wind rose. There was a smell of salt and fish on the air.

They left their bicycles against the railing and wandered along the streets looking in shop windows. Colourful windmills twirled in the breeze outside a shop, where wooden spades and tin buckets hung from the door. Patsy took a threepenny bit from her purse and bought a red windmill, which she held high in the air. It twirled crazily as they turned the corner that led back to the main street. They met Karen coming out of the baker's shop.

'I was wondering what to get for tea,' she said, heading for the grocer's.

'I'm starving,' John said.

'Me too,' added Patsy. 'We passed a fish and chip shop.'

'Smelt delicious.'

'Fish and chips it is then. Now I must get some messages.'

It was the first time John had had a companion of his own age with whom to share his summer holidays, and it was the first holiday Patsy had ever been on. The cottage had two bedrooms at the top of a small staircase. Patsy slept in a bed in the bay window of Karen's room. John had a room to himself. They were tired from the journey and the change of air, and slept soundly.

After breakfast they took a picnic to a beach half-a-mile away, along a dirt track, overgown with gorse and brambles. As Karen settled herself on a rug and got out her book, John and Patsy put on their swimming togs and ran to the edge of the water, splashing in the waves. Patsy sat down and yelped as the icy waves washed over her. Karen came to paddle her feet, and cautioned Patsy not to stay in for too long.

The few days passed quickly. On the last day they cycled along the coast road, buying fresh cod for supper on the way back. Karen packed when the children were in bed. Later she walked down to the quay to gaze at the silent sea. As she watched the sun set in a blaze of orange, she wished they did not have to leave. The last few days had been the happiest she had known for years. Now she must go home and face the heartbreak of taking John to boarding school, before returning to America with Hank, for how long she did not know.

Thinking of Hank and America, she shivered. How could she tell him that she did not want to go back with him? She had come to rely on him. He made all the decisions. It was easier to let him think for her than to have to think for herself. Since Paul's death, she seemed incapable of taking charge of her own life. She wished she had the strength to live on her own with John, to do what she wanted to do. But her judgment was clouded by fear, and she was afraid to take responsibility for herself and her child. Perhaps if she postponed her trip until Christmas, she thought, John would be settled well in school. Pulling her cardigan around her shoulders, she retraced her steps, wishing that she could stay in Nancy's little cottage with John forever, and not have to face the complications of her life.

Karen drove John to Saint Clement's boarding school, County Kildare, in Bill's car. They hardly exchanged a word on the journey. John, too numb to speak, stared ahead, and Karen kept her eyes on the road. As the car reached its destination, John began to tremble.

'You won't forget to write soon?' Karen's voice was too bright.

'No.'

'If there's anything you want, let me know. You have the phone number safely in your stationery box.'

'Yes.'

'Don't expect too much too soon, darling. You won't settle in straight away. Give it a chance.'

He did not answer her.

As they drove through the gates, he stared ahead, eyes fixed on the iron fire escape that ran down the side of the ugly grey building. Two older boys came to take his trunk.

Karen hugged him. 'Take care of yourself. Don't forget to say your prayers.'

John swallowed a lump in his throat as his eyes misted over.

'Bye,' he sniffed.

'I'll miss you.' Karen's voice was strangled.

A tall boy approached. 'Are you John Thornton?'

'Yes.'

'My name is James Lacey. I'll take you to your dorm.'

'Thank you,' Karen said.

'Don't worry, Mrs Thornton, we'll take good care of him.' He put his arm on John's shoulder.

John shook it off and, without looking at his mother, moved away.

Inside the building they met groups of boys huddled at the foot of the wide staircase, on the landing, and in the long corridors they passed along to get to the dormitory.

'This is your bed,' James said. 'When you have it made up, I'll take you to meet the Form Master. You've only got a quarter of an hour, so hurry up.'

John looked startled. 'I don't know how to make a bed.'

'Well you'd better learn then, because that's what you'll have to do every morning for the rest of your time here.'

He opened John's trunk, which the boys had left at the end of his bed, removed the sheets and blankets and showed him what to do.

'There's a list of rules on the inside of your locker. You get a mark against you if you break one of them.' John read them.

1. No talking, or running in the corridor.

2. No talking in the Dormitory, especially after lights out.

3. No food allowed in the Dormitory.

4. No swearing or taking the name of the Lord in vain.

'Get a move on. You'll be late for the meeting with the Form Master.'

Outside the Form Master's study, a row of new boys were sitting on chairs. John took his place and waited. Nobody spoke.

Eventually the Form Master came out, a grey-haired

man, wearing a black gown. He removed his glasses to look at them.

'Welcome to Saint Clement's,' he said. 'I hope you'll all be happy here.'

John looked at him in amazement. 'I won't be happy here,' he said. 'I want to go home.'

Someone sniggered. The Form Master frowned, then smiled at John. 'That's what you think today. Believe me, you'll settle down in time. Soon you'll have forgotten all about home.'

'No I won't.' John's face was red.

'Ahem. Well, we'll see.' He glanced at his notes. 'What we expect from our boys is courage, hard work and a community spirit. Our aim is to produce good citizens, men fit to take their place in the world, young men worthy of our school. You can count on us to look after your welfare. All we expect in return is your cooperation. If you have any problems, come and see me. That's what I'm here for. You have each been assigned a fifth-year student to show you the ropes and help you settle in. I wish you well and will see you individually during the week.'

A bell clanged, echoing through the building. The Form Master looked at his watch. 'Time for afternoon tea,' he said. 'Go quietly to the Refectory.'

The Refectory was a vast room, full of boys pushing, shoving and shouting to one another above the noise and clatter of crockery.

'So you're not going to be happy here?'

John turned and found himself looking up into the red face of a heavyset boy, who seemed to be bursting out of his uniform.

'You heard me, Sprat,' he continued. 'Cat got your tongue?'

'I d-on't kn-ow you.' John flushed as he stumbled over the words.

'Don't worry about that. You'll get to know us soon enough. We'll guarantee your misery. Won't we, lads?' The boys next to him laughed in chorus.

'Come on.' James appeared and pushed John forward, calling to the bully boy to leave him alone.

John helped himself to his allocation of two buns, and took his place at the long wooden table, with the rest of the new boys. No one spoke to him, for which he was grateful. He thought of Patsy and what he would say in his letter to her. Remembering Gertie's tears when he had said goodbye to her, and the crisp new pound note Gran had put in his pocket, made the tears trickle down his cheeks. He lowered his head to hide them.

That night he slept between cold sheets in the silent dormitory. He was lonely. It was obvious from the bewildered look on the other new boys' faces that they felt lonely too. The rule of silence made it impossible for them to get to know one another. The following day he sat in the classroom as Mr Fahy, the Maths and Latin teacher, began Latin declensions. John, hating the subject instantly, tried to concentrate.

Something whizzed past his ear. Suddenly, a roll of paper landed on his desk. He turned in time to catch a wink from the boy in the opposite desk. Cautiously he opened up the paper. It read, 'I hate it here too. My name is Andrew Foley.'

John nodded and smiled at him.

'John Thornton, please stand and repeat what I have just said.' John looked up to see Mr Fahy staring at him.

'I didn't hear what you were saying, sir,' said John, slowly rising.

'And why? Because you weren't paying attention. Write out one hundred times, "I must pay attention in class". Now sit down.'

'Yes, sir.'

After class, Andrew said, 'Sorry. That was tough luck.'

John shrugged. 'I couldn't understand what he was saying anyway.'

'I'm looking forward to rugby practice. Do you play?'

'No. I suppose I could learn.'

'Put your name down. Give it a try.'

That afternoon they ran together to the rugby pitch, and tossed Andrew's ball back and forth to one another. John liked the feel of the ball. He was also fond of Andrew. By the time Mr Miller, the Games Master, arrived and lined them all up to take their names, he realised that he had not thought of home for almost an hour.

September crawled slowly into October. The trees in the avenue shed their leaves, the grounds of the school looked bare and dismal. Days grew shorter. The boys chased the rugby ball around the sodden playing fields, Mr Miller's cries dying on the wind. John did not mind the mud on his boots. He was enjoying the game. Soon he would be going home for the half-term break.

14

It was half-term break and the commotion downstairs woke John up. He sneaked out of bed and, kneeling against the banisters of the landing, looked down the stairwell. Gertie was talking to someone on the telephone. Her voice was high-pitched and excited. She called to Bill to come quickly.

Bill rushed into the hall.

Gertie put her hand over the receiver. 'They think they've found Paul.'

'Who?'

'The Red Cross.'

'Here, let me talk to them.'

Bill took the receiver. 'What's all this about?' he asked. There was silence while he listened. Eventually he thanked whoever was at the other end of the line, and replaced the receiver.

'It sounds as if it's Paul,' he told Gertie. 'They think they may have found him.'

'That's what the woman from the tracing agency said. Should we tell Karen they think they've found him? It would be cruel if it turned out not to be him. She's been through enough, and so have his parents.'

'I think it's our duty to tell Karen.'

'It could break her heart.'

'She should go to him. Where is he?'

'They've brought him to some hospital near Portsmouth. I can't remember exactly what she said. Anyway what's the point in telling Karen until we're absolutely certain that it's him? She said they would write once they know.'

'I suppose you're right.'

They were talking about his father. Supposing he was waiting somewhere to be identified, and because Gertie refused to tell Karen, he would have to stay there for the rest of his life? Surely his father would want to see him? He went back to bed and lay still for a long time, wondering what to do. Should he tell his mother when she returned from seeing Hank off at Shannon Airport? What would Hank say? 'Anything to cause a sensation,' that's what he would say. Suddenly John had an idea. He would ask Anthony what to do. Anthony knew all about England, and the people who lived there. Anthony knew a lot of things.

Gertie did not mention the phone call to John when he came down to breakfast the next morning. She was so quiet, he began to wonder if he had been dreaming.

Mrs Keogh was polishing the hall table when John came up from the breakfast room. The doorbell rang. Mick, the postman, handed her an enormous parcel.

'For the young lad,' he said. 'From America.' Mrs Keogh looked over the parcel. 'It's from his grandparents. He'll be thrilled. It's his birthday next week. Did you hear the news?'

John slid into the jamb of the sitting-room door.

'No. What?'

'They think they've found his father.'

'Whose father?'

'John's father.'

'I didn't know he had one.'

'Remember the chap who went missing during the war?'

'Karen's husband?'

'The very one.'

'That's ten years ago. Sure John wasn't even born.'

'Well he's turned up and there's murder.'

'Why? They should be delighted.'

'It's not that simple. Karen's involved with his cousin Hank now.'

'The big American who was here?'

'They're planning on getting married.'

'Janey, I see the problem.'

'And now they're wondering what's wrong with the husband that he didn't show up long before this.' She spat on her cloth and polished the brass door knocker.

'Could be anything. You know Bertie Moran, sells the newspapers, head always gyrating?'

Mrs Keogh nodded.

'They say he got shell-shocked in the war.'

John sneaked back downstairs and knocked at Mrs Quinn's door.

Mrs Quinn was feeding Martin, the baby. 'Patsy's at school, love. She won't be back until after three o'clock.'

Damien was pushing a toy lorry full of dirty bricks around the room. Big cardboard boxes lined the walls. The rest of the room was empty, except for the table and chairs.

'Are you leaving?'

'The new house'll be ready to move into the day after tomorrow.'

'Where's Anthony?'

'In bed. He has a practice fight tonight. A run-up to the big fight in England.'

'Can I see him?'

'Is there something wrong?'

'No, nothing. Tell him I called down to ask him something.'

The look of disappointment in his face made her say, 'Wait a minute, I'll see if he's awake.'

He heard her footsteps on the concrete floor and Anthony's voice saying, 'What time is it?' Then she called John into the room.

'What's wrong?' Anthony yawned and shook himself awake.

'They've found my father. At least they think they have,' John whispered.

'Who have?' Anthony sat bolt upright.

'The Red Cross I think. But I heard Bill saying that he didn't think it was right to tell my mother. Then Mrs Keogh told the postman just now.' John began to cry.

'Calm down.'

'Why don't they want to find him?'

Anthony was thoughtful. 'They don't want any trouble.'

'What kind of trouble?'

'I don't know. What did Gertie tell you?'

'Nothing. She mustn't want me to know.'

'Did you let on you heard anything?'

'No.'

John began to cry again.

'Cut that out,' Anthony said roughly.

John stopped. Finally he said in a flat voice, 'I'm going to find him. I've thought about it all night.' He was desperate.

Anthony said, 'It won't work.' Then his face brightened as he muttered, more to himself than to John, 'Still, it might work. I'll do some thinking and call up to you later.'

'Thanks, Anthony.'

'Hey, where do they keep their letters?'

'In the glove compartment in the hall stand.'

'Watch out for that letter from the Red Cross. Let me know when it comes.'

Gertie was quiet all that day. Bill came home from work with a Dinky toy for John.

As Mrs Keogh was leaving, she said to Gertie, 'I'll call into the church on me way home. Say a novena for missing persons.'

'Be quiet,' Gertie hissed.

'Missing souls I mean,' she corrected herself and left hurriedly.

Patsy came up with a note from Anthony. 'Meet me in the coach house at eight sharp. Don't talk to anyone,' it said.

'What's up?' Patsy asked. 'Is it a secret?'

'What are you talking about?'

'Mammy said you were looking for me this morning.'

'Just thought you might have stayed home from school. We could have played a game of soldiers.'

'I told you I'm not missing any more school. It's amazing that she let me go on holidays with you. I don't want to have to stay behind a year.'

'You don't know how lucky you are. I wish I was kept back a year. Anyway tell Anthony—' John stopped.

'What?' Patsy prompted.

He glanced at the note again. 'Nothing.'

That evening Anthony waited for John in the coach house.

'Let's go upstairs,' Anthony said when he arrived. 'We don't want any nosy parkers listening to us.'

Once upstairs, he shut the door, and leaned against it.

'How much money do you have?'

'Two pounds.'

'It's not a lot.'

'It's my pocket money for the term.'

'Supposing I take you to London with me to look for your father. Could you get your hands on more dough?'

'Would you really take me with you?'

'That's what I said.'

'Why?'

'Because I feel sorry for you. You don't know whether you're coming or going, with your mother always away. I bet you haven't a friend in that posh boarding school. The big lads probably pick on you.'

John was trembling.

'I think it would be good for you to find your father. You need him. The rest of them seem to be managing fine without him.'

Tears flooded John's eyes and his shoulders shook. He turned away, his hands covering his face, ashamed of Anthony seeing him cry so much.

'You've got to promise me some things first,' Anthony said.

'Yeh.'

'There are certain rules you'll have to follow.'

'OK.'

'You'll do whatever I tell you to do, no matter what.' He began pacing the floor. 'I won't be interested in hearing that you're tired, or weak, or any of that claptrap. I'm not going to look for your father to impress you. I'm doing it because I think you should be the one to find him, and—' he stopped and smiled self-consciously, 'the adventurous side of it appeals to me. You'll have to be able to sleep anywhere, stay awake when you have to, eat whatever there is. In other words, you'll be living rough for a few days.'

John wiped his eyes. 'I'll do anything you say.'

'Another thing. If we don't find your father, you won't crack up on me.'

'I promise.'

'Now, we have to make a plan so that you can be gone for a while before they start looking for you. When do you have to go back to school?'

'Sunday evening.'

'I'll tell Gertie that Mr Murphy is going to bring you to Kildare.'

'And is he?'

'No. But then neither are you. You'll be in England before you're missed. To be on the safe side, I'll get Biddy

213

to phone the school to say that you have the flu and won't be back for a few days. Now get going while I make my plans.'

15

Anthony told his mother he would be late home, and went down to Mulgrave Street to call for Spud. Spud was working in his father's fruit and vegetable shop. Even though he was under age, his father let him drive the delivery van. Sometimes after work, Spud liked to dress up in his good suit, slip away in the van, and drive the lads around. Sometimes they would drive to the fish and chipper, take it in turns to buy chips, and eat them at the seafront, watching people walking past. At other times they would drive to Biddy Plunkett's house to collect her. They would shout at girls as they drove past, or occasionally drop in to see friends of Biddy's. Biddy was working in the Roman Café afternoons and evenings.

'You can't just stand there,' she said when they came in, and did not order anything. 'You'll have to order something.'

'What'll ye have, Anto?' Spud pulled a ten shilling note from his pocket and slapped it down on the counter.

'I'll have a lemonade, seeing as you're paying.'

Biddy brought the drinks to the table. She smiled and nodded to the customers as they came in. She had created a happy atmosphere for herself in the café and was good at her job. Biddy liked the noise, and enjoyed swaggering around with a tray full of coffee, tea and cakes.

After closing time, Anthony and Spud sat waiting for her to finish cleaning up. Anthony watched her washing dishes, piling them up on the counter, drying them and wiping down the sink. He was comforted by the intimacy of her movements. At times like this he forgot the other side of himself, the side that craved a rich life, and yearned to be somewhere else – that side of him that would risk his future on a sudden impulse.

One of the customers, surly and aggressive, refused to leave. When the manager pointed out that the café was closing, he latched on to Biddy, following her around and talking to her. She continued washing dishes, head averted, movements steady, her neat plaits resting on her shoulders.

Anthony called out to the man, 'It's time you went home'. Then he went and stood beside him.

'Time to go home,' he repeated and walked him to the door.

At the door the man said, 'Are you trying to get rid of me?' His voice was dangerous.

Anthony grabbed him, and punched him hard in the chest and on the nose. Blood spurted from his nose.

Anthony caught him as his knees buckled. He carried him outside and sat him up against the wall of the café. Biddy was crying when he returned.

'You enjoyed that, didn't you?'

'What do you mean?'

'I saw the excitement in your face when you punched that poor eejit. You were agitating for a fight.'

'Rubbish. He was making a nuisance of himself. I was only protecting you.'

Biddy shook her head. 'There's fighting in your blood and it frightens me.'

'Come on,' Spud called. 'Let's get out of here.'

Anthony's eyes were on Biddy's face. 'You'd have been more frightened if that fellow had made a pass at you.'

'I can take care of myself,' Biddy shouted.

'I dunno.' Anthony was exasperated. 'You try to do a good turn and it only lands you in trouble. I'm off.'

'I'll be ready in a minute.'

'We'll be waiting in the van.'

Biddy eventually came out, her coat over her arm, calling goodnight to the manager. They drove around aimlessly. Anthony sat in the back seat, too restless from the fight with the customer to want to go home.

Spud said, 'Let's go over to Reilly's.'

Reilly had a sister who was pretty. Anthony knew that Spud liked her, although he had never said so.

'It's late.' Biddy said. 'They might be in bed.'

'No harm tryin'.' Spud ran down to the basement and rang the bell.

The door opened and Reilly beckoned to them to come in. Reilly was alone.

'I was sorting through a pile of old records to see what I could sell. I'm skint.'

'You're not the only one. I've an invitation to fight in London, and haven't the dough to go there.' Anthony's voice held a note of gloom.

Reilly's sister came down the stairs. Spud slowly moved out to the passageway. 'Hello, Eileen,' he said in the soft voice he reserved for girls.

'Hello, Spud. I came down to see if any of you would like a cup of Irel coffee?'

'What I wouldn't give for a cup of Irel,' Biddy said as Eileen came into the room.

'I'll put the kettle on.'

'I'll help you make it.' Spud followed her out of the room.

When they had left, Anthony said to Biddy, 'I have a problem'.

'What's new about that?'

'It's a new problem.'

'Tell us.'

'It's confidential.'

'We won't tell anyone,' Biddy said. 'Cross our hearts and hope to die.'

'John's father has been found.'

'What? After all these years?'

'Where?' Spud asked, as he came back into the room.

'The south coast of England.'

'I always thought he was dead.' Reilly was uninterested.

'So did John's mother and the rest of the Doyle family by the looks of it.'

'How did you find out?' Biddy asked.

'John told me. He overheard Gertie and Bill. To make a long story short, I said I'd help him. The kid's upset.'

'Of course he's upset. What'd you expect?' Biddy said.

'The trouble is, it costs money to get to England, and he doesn't have much.' He lowered his voice. 'And I haven't any.'

'I'll lend you my savings,' Biddy said.

'You can borrow my tent,' Reilly offered.

'Wait.' Anthony raised his hands. 'It's not as simple as that. I have to make a plan. I'd want to make a few quid out of this trip. Enough to get me to the fight in London. Kill two birds with the one stone.'

Reilly said, 'Why don't you rob a bank?'

'Very funny.'

'I've a better idea,' Spud said. 'Rob the grannie. That oul one is worth a fortune. She's always winnin' on the horses.'

'How do you know?'

'Doesn't me father put her bets on on the q.t. If Gertie found out, she'd slice into her. Gertie can be very tough.'

'Has to be. She doesn't have it easy either. How she puts up with that Mrs Keogh I'll never know.'

'She won't have to put up with her much longer. I hear Father Breen is takin' her on as his housekeeper.'

'God help poor Father Breen, that's all I can say.'

'This isn't sorting out the problem of finding John's father,' Anthony said.

'The best thing to do is to try to find out exactly what they were told.'

Anthony shook his head. 'How'll I do that?'

'I know,' Biddy said. 'Ask the granny.'

'She's dotin',' Spud said.

'No she isn't. That one's as sharp as a blade. She only pretends to be doting, but she knows everything that goes on in that house.'

'I'll think about it.'

Afterwards Anthony walked Biddy home along the seafront. The night sky was black over the sea. They were both silent. Anthony was thinking of his plan. He would borrow ten pounds from John's grandmother. That would not be difficult if he pretended he had a tip from Spud's father. Reilly's tent would be useful to take, and his flask. A photograph of Paul would be useful to have. John could get that.

Biddy was thinking of John's dream of finding his

father. She believed in dreams, even the dreams of others. She felt that outside influences were at work and that this was a directive from God – an answer to the millions of prayers and masses that had been offered up over the years for Paul's safe return. Not for a second did she believe that Anthony was doing anything wrong. He was an instrument in this whole plan, a chosen messenger. It was predestined. She imagined Paul in a safe place, somewhere more accessible than heaven, speaking in a shy voice, looking eternally young. The whole idea cemented her belief in Anthony's superhuman qualities. After all, he had been picked by God.

'You won't mind if I don't take you to London with me this time?'

' 'Course not.'

'I'll make it up to you. I'll win the fight in London. That should be worth a few bob. I'll bring you back a new dress.'

Biddy squeezed his hand. 'I don't want a new dress.'

'What would you like?'

They stood looking at the sea.

'I'd like you to come back safe. Not with your head split open.'

Gertie had gone to ten o'clock mass and Gran was sitting up in bed knitting when Anthony knocked on her bedroom door.

221

'Come in,' she called.

Anthony poked his head round the door. 'Hello, Granny Doyle. How are you this morning?'

If Gran was surprised, she did not show it. 'As you see me. Sick.'

'That's too bad. Mrs Doyle sent me up to know if you'd like a cup of tea.'

'I'm sick of tea. Would it ever occur to her to send someone up to ask me if I'd like a drop of brandy?'

Anthony moved further into the room. 'Would you like a drop of brandy?'

Gran glared at him. 'What do you think? An old woman like me needs somethin' stronger than tea to warm her bones. Anyway, where would you get brandy?'

'In the off-licence. Mr Toner knows me well.'

'You don't drink, do you?'

'No, Mrs Doyle. 'Course I don't drink, but I sometimes get a baby Power for me mother.'

'I see. I suppose it'd be no harm. Give me that bag over there.'

Anthony passed her the handbag.

'How is your mother?' she asked as she searched for her purse.

'Fine, Mrs Doyle. Sent me up to ask after your health.'

'She knows the state of me health. More in her line to come up and see me herself.'

'She's busy with the baby.'

'Get me a naggin of brandy, and don't tell them downstairs.' She handed Anthony a ten shilling note.

Anthony took the money.' 'Course I won't.' He paused, then said casually, 'I hear Mr Tom is tipped to win tomorrow.'

'Who told you that?'

'Spud's father.'

'I didn't know there was a race on tomorrow. I must check the newspaper.'

'I'll look it up for you. He's putting on a tenner.' Anthony concentrated on the wall above her head.

'A tenner.'

'He says it's a certainty.'

Gran was thoughtful. 'Unless he breaks a leg.'

'Not a chance.'

'Funny. Spud's father didn't mention it to me.'

'He forgot. That's why he sent me.'

'I see. Well I'm not puttin' a tenner on a horse. Against me principles. I'll put two pounds on. That's me highest bet.' She gave him two pounds. 'Don't forget the change from the brandy. How's the boxin'? Are you goin' to London?' Gran added.

'I was hoping to go. But I don't think so.'

'Why?'

'No money.'

'That's a shame. How much do you need?' Anthony pretended to calculate. 'About a tenner.'

'I see.' Gran studied him. 'You've done well, Anthony.

Turned into a nice lad. You owe Mr Murphy and the boxin' a lot.'

'I know, Mrs Doyle.'

'I'll lend you the money.'

'Would you? That'd be great. Only I'd have to win the fight to be able to pay you back.'

'You'll win the fight all right. Call back tomorrow and I'll have it for you.'

'Thanks, Mrs Doyle, you're a star. I'll say a prayer that you'll be better soon.'

'Don't worry about the prayers. Look after yourself and stay out of trouble.'

'I will.'

'And, Anthony?'

'Yes?'

'Don't tell lies. You'll always get found out in the end.'

Anthony's face reddened. 'Yes, Granny Doyle.'

Anthony hovered around the hall waiting for Mrs Keogh to finish polishing the stair-rods. When she was gone, he went to the glove compartment in the hall stand and lifted the lid. Pulling out the bundle of letters he knew he would find there, he shoved them inside his lumber jacket, and left quickly.

Back in his room he searched through them until he found the letter with a red cross on the envelope, addressed to Karen. He opened it.

We wish to inform you that Flight Commander Paul Thornton, missing in action, presumed dead, has been located. Please contact us as soon as possible.

His mother was calling him.

'Coming,' he called, shoving the bundle of letters in the crevice behind the shutters of the windows.

John lay in bed, fully clothed, waiting for the clock to strike ten. He heard Gertie and Bill coming upstairs, their door closing. When he thought they were in bed, he got up, put on his warm socks and boots and crept downstairs. Opening the window, he climbed out onto the sill, and caught the bar of the bridge outside the back door to support him, while he swung his legs onto it. Once outside, he leaned back and closed the window carefully, then cautiously made his way up the garden path. He felt calm and anonymous in the dark. The coach house was empty. He stamped his feet while he waited for Anthony, feeling for the first time the relief of not having to go back to school, and the excitement of the search for his father.

His father would be so delighted to see him that he would want to be with him all the time. He took the photograph of his father out of his pocket, and, although he could not see it clearly, he said to it, 'I'll find you, Dad, and, whatever happens, I'll stay with you for the rest of my life.' Suddenly all the misery of being separated from his father overwhelmed him, and he had to make a conscious effort not to cry. He blew his warm breath into his hands and rubbed them together while he waited. Then he heard a crunching noise.

'Are you there?' Anthony hissed.

John moved forward.

'Come on. Let's go.' Anthony moved swiftly to the high wall at the end of the garden, and clambered up it. John followed, glad of his strong boots to help him climb, and Anthony's supporting hand, when he reached the top. As his eyes grew accustomed to the darkness, he saw the shape of Spud's van waiting down the lane. 'Psst – follow me.' Anthony leapt to the ground and waited while John felt along the wall for crevices to put his hands and feet into. When he felt secure, he swung himself over the top, and dropped down on the other side. The beam of Anthony's torch led them down the muddy lane, past trees that lurked like evil giants in the dark. They got into the car.

'At last,' Spud murmured and started the engine before they had shut the doors.

As the car moved slowly away, John leaned back into his seat. A wave of unease swept over him. Supposing Gran went into his room, as she sometimes did, and found that he was not there.

The comforting sound of the engine taking them nearer to the boat and the familiar smell of Anthony's Woodbine calmed him. He had to remind himself that they were not running away from home. They were on a secret mission to search for his father.

The mail boat lay peacefully in the harbour waiting for its passengers. Anthony bought a ticket, and engaged the ticket man in conversation while John sneaked on ahead, so that the ticket man would not see him. He ran up the gangplank and took the stairs two at a time until he had reached the higher level, as they had planned. He hid in a corner of the upper deck and waited for Anthony. It began to rain. When he heard footsteps approaching, he froze with fear. The footsteps stopped, then retreated. Stealthily he carried on, groping his way across ropes, grabbing poles. When he found a lifeboat, he hid in it and waited.

The boat pulled slowly away from the quayside. John watched the trail of lights along the coast diminishing into the distance, as the boat slipped between the piers, and turned right for Holyhead. A cold wind blew across the Irish Sea. He huddled down into his coat, breathing in the smell of the sea, and listened to the chug of the engines churning up the waves. What was keeping Anthony? Maybe he had met someone. Had he been stopped by the Guards? He sank down further into his coat. If he had been warm, he would have fallen asleep. He concentrated on being a stowaway on a ship, rather than a very tired boy, in a boat, feeling lost.

As soon as he heard the low familiar whistle, he slipped

out of the lifeboat and called, 'Over here,' into the darkness. Anthony stood there, head bent against the wind.

'Are you all right?'

'Yes.'

'I've brought you a hot drink.'

'Thanks.' John wrapped his hands around the mug of tea.

'All I could get.' He pulled a packet of Marietta biscuits from his pocket.

'Is anyone looking for us?'

'No one suspects a thing. When you've finished your tea, get back in the lifeboat and I'll cover you with this tarpaulin. It'll keep you dry and warm. I'll give you a shout when we get nearer to Holyhead.'

John slept and woke alternately as the boat rolled over the waves. His stomach felt queasy. He fell asleep again. The next time he woke, Anthony was beside him.

'We're nearly there. Come on.'

The sea was pitch black, with only a few lights in the distance. 'That's Holyhead.'

Once on shore, Anthony bought a ticket, then elbowed John to move ahead and they lost themselves among the queue for the London train. As they boarded the train, the crowds engulfed them.

'This is great.' Anthony pushed his way ahead. 'Sit next to the window,' he told John and seated himself opposite.

The train was packed. John crouched into the corner, counting the droplets of rain chasing one another down the window pane, as the train rocked from side to side through the stillness of the night.

When Anthony saw the ticket man approaching he whispered to John, 'Hide in the toilet'.

John excused himself and went in the opposite direction to the ticket man. He waited in the toilet until someone banged the door and shouted, 'Will ye hurry up. I'm burstin' '.

He returned to his seat and finally fell asleep. Anthony shook him. 'We're in London.'

John woke. 'That wasn't much of a journey.'

'You were asleep.'

The woman next to John looked at them curiously. 'Somebody expecting you?' she asked.

'Our auntie is expecting us,' Anthony said. Seeing the doubtful expression on her face, he added, 'My uncle will be at the station to meet us.'

'That's good.' She glanced at John. 'London is so vast, and dangerous.'

Suddenly John was afraid. He kept his eyes on Anthony, knowing it was safer to say nothing.

At Euston station John slid past the ticket collector while Anthony handed him his ticket.

' 'Ere! Where do you think you're going?' The ticket collector reached out to grab John, who wriggled out of his grasp, and dodged through the crowds.

'I'll catch him.' Anthony sprinted away from the irate ticket collector and caught up with John.

'Follow me,' he called out to him and together they ran as fast as they could, until they were out of sight. A bus took them to Marble Arch in the West End. Anthony settled back in his seat to watch the busy city. 'I've never seen so much traffic, and it's only six o'clock in the morning. This is the place for me,' he added. 'Everything moving, not like sleepy Dun Laoghaire.'

'Don't you ever get tired?' John's voice was weak with fatigue.

'Nope. I'm fit.' He flexed his muscles. 'You'll have to take up boxing when you're older. Build up your strength.'

They walked down Oxford Street, gazing in shop windows as they went.

'I thought Dublin was big, but I've never seen anything like this!' John exclaimed.

'Stick by me or you'll get lost.'

They wandered all over the place, and bought sweets and lemonade when it occured to them that they were hungry.

Eventually Anthony asked a man selling ice-cream cones what bus to get to Portsmouth.

'The bus at the far side of the road will take you to Woking. You could catch a train from there.'

Anthony looked hesitant.

'Can't afford it?' the man asked.

Anthony nodded his head.

'You could always hitch a lift on the motorway once you get to Woking.' The man filled two cones to the brim and handed them one each.

'That'll keep the wolf from the door,' he said, refusing to take the money Anthony offered him.

'Thank you,' they said in unison.

They took the bus to Woking, and made their way to the road signposted for Portsmouth. Anthony thumbed every passing vehicle. Finally a truck stopped.

'Portsmouth?' Anthony asked.

'Near enough,' the driver called down.

Clambering up into the truck, they squeezed themselves in beside the driver, an enormous man who took up most of the bench seat.

'I have a few stops along the way,' he said.

'That's all right,' Anthony said.

'On holiday?'

'Business,' Anthony replied brusquely.

The truck driver laughed. 'What kind of business?'

'Boxing business.' John could feel the vexation in Anthony's voice.

'I used to box. Still follow the game.'

Anthony perked up. 'I came over to compete in the Amateur Junior Championships in London.'

'Portsmouth's a bit out of your way, innit?'

'We promised our auntie we'd visit her, didn't we?' Anthony said without hesitation, looking at John.

231

'Yes,' John said meekly.

They talked for a while about boxing. John remained silent, watching the countryside rush past, fascinated with the red buses and red pillar boxes. They stopped often, while the driver made his food deliveries to the shops.

'You boys must be hungry,' he said. 'We'll stop at Joe's for a bite to eat.'

Having bought them a meal of sausages and chips, the truck driver let them out on the outskirts of Portsmouth.

'It's too dark to search for the nursing home now,' Anthony said.

They pitched their makeshift tent in a sheltered corner of a field, and lay awake in the dark listening to the rising wind and the waves crashing in the sea. Beneath the sound of the storm, Anthony heard John crying.

'What's up?'

'I'm tired . . . hungry . . . I dunno.'

'You mean you wish you were at home.'

'Yeh.'

'You've forgotten the rule. No moaning. It's too late now anyway. Get some sleep. You'll feel better in the morning. Here, have this.' He rummaged in his bag and passed John a bar of chocolate.

The sky was bitter and grey when they awoke. Anthony broke off some overhanging branches and built a fire. He made tea with the water from his flask. They packed up and moved soundlessly along Clarence Esplanade. Anthony stopped to admire the anchor, a relic of Lord Nelson's flagship, *HMS Victory*. John grew impatient. They continued past derelict buildings, bombed during the war, now in the process of reconstruction. At the junction of King's Road, a newspaper man was setting up his stall for the day. They asked for directions.

He pointed left. 'It's probably The Elms, Elm Grove, you're looking for. Posh end. Can't miss it. Big house.'

They passed along the tree-lined avenue of Victorian houses. Dogs barked behind gates. Finally they came to the largest house, barricaded behind a high wall, its wrought-iron gates padlocked.

'This is it.'

'It can't be. It's locked.'

'It says "The Elms" on the gatepost. Maybe they lock it at night. I'm not waiting around here.'

Anthony shinned up the wall and sat on it, extending his hand to help John up. When John had safely reached the top, Anthony dropped effortlessly down on the other side and motioned to John to do the same. John jumped, but fell as he landed. He got up without a word and followed Anthony along the avenue to the front door. They walked slowly up the steps. Anthony lifted the brass knocker and let it fall once. John stood in the cold sunlight, shifting his weight from one foot to the other. When he heard footsteps approaching the door, his face turned bright red and he looked at Anthony for support. Anthony winked at him.

A woman in uniform stood there, a look of disapproval on her colourless face. Her cold eyes stared from one to the other.

'Yes?'

'I'd like to speak to someone in charge, please,' said Anthony.

'What is it in connection with?' Her voice was as chilly as her eyes.

Anthony produced the letter from the Red Cross.

16

She took the letter and told them to wait. They hesitated at the door, then took a few tentative steps into the spacious hall, at the end of which was a beautiful curved staircase. The woman came back and led them up the stairs, to a room lined with books.

They waited, not knowing whether to sit down or stay standing. Before they could decide, a thickset man with horn-rimmed glasses came into the room, the letter from the Red Cross in his hand.

'Hello, boys.' He studied Anthony first, then John as he took a seat behind his desk. 'My name is Pettigrew. I'm in charge here. What can I do for you?'

Anthony cleared his throat. 'We think, that is we have information from—' He cleared his throat again. 'Do you have a fighter pilot named Paul Thornton here?'

Mr Pettigrew gave Anthony a long appraising look, as though he had become worthy enough to merit his attention. Carefully he read the letter and returned it to its envelope.

'I'm afraid we have no one by that name here.'

'Have you anyone who looks like this?' John took the photograph of his father from his pocket, and handed it to Mr Pettigrew, who studied it. 'I don't know this man,' he said finally.

'He's my father,' John said.

John's eyes were puffy and there was a dirt streak down the side of his face, which Anthony cursed himself for not noticing before.

'His father went missing during the war. John was only a baby,' Anthony said.

'Did you came all the way from Ireland to find him, even though you never saw the man in your life?'

'We thought he might be here,' John said.

'If he is, I can assure you he won't look anything like this photograph.'

'Sorry to have wasted your time.' Anthony reached out for the letter and put it in his pocket.

Turning his inquisitorial gaze on Anthony, Mr Pettigrew said, 'On the contrary, I admire young fellows with guts. It can't be easy traipsing around with such flimsy information to go on.'

'We had better go then,' Anthony said to John. 'Come on.'

Mr Pettigrew was watching them. 'You must be hungry. Follow me and I'll get you something to eat.' He smiled at them for the first time.

He took them to the kitchen, where rows of stainless

steel trays, laid for breakfast, were waiting to be delivered to the patients.

'Good morning, Gladys,' he said to a woman who was stirring a saucepan at the stove.

'Mornin', Mr P. What can I get you?'

'These boys are hungry. Would you give them some breakfast, please?'

'Certainly. What would you like? Bacon, eggs, sausage, fried bread?'

Anthony's eyes shone. 'Yes please.'

'Take a seat.' He sat them down at the corner of a long scrubbed table. 'I want you to learn something from this experience. Don't go on any wild goose chases until you have more positive information. I'd advise you to abandon your search, and return to your homes.'

Gladys set the table and Mr Pettigrew said, 'Enjoy your breakfast, boys. When you've finished, Gladys will show you out.'

He shook hands with them both and left.

'There's something fishy about him,' Anthony said under his breath. 'Something's up.'

'What?'

'I dunno. I'm trying to work it out.'

'Have you been here long?' he asked Gladys as she cooked their breakfast.

'Too long,' she sighed. 'One of these days I'll be mistaken for one of the patients, I'm gettin' that forgetful.'

'Are the patients forgetful?' John asked.

'You could say that, considerin' most of them don't know who they are in the first place. I know them all. Not by their real names, but the names they were given when they came here.'

'Were they given new identities?'

'Sort of. I suppose they had to be given names to distinguish them from one another. Poor souls.' John took the photograph from his pocket.

'Have you ever seen this man?'

Gladys put on her glasses and looked at the photograph. She shook her head. 'No, but there was a man here a few weeks ago askin' questions, and he had that same photograph.'

'Who was he?'

'Couldn't say. Mr Pettigrew knew him. He stayed for lunch and they had a long chat. Funny he didn't tell you. Perhaps it would be better not to ask him. He has a strict rule about what information he gives out about his patients.'

'Why?'

'To protect them. That's why they're here. They can't protect themselves against the outside world. Oh, the evils of war.'

'Is there any other nursing home like this one in the area?' Anthony asked, assuming a businesslike air.

'There's the Royal Naval Hospital in Gosport. That's where the majority of them were sent.'

When they had finished eating, Anthony and John

thanked Gladys and said goodbye. Mr Pettigrew was talking on the telephone in the hall. Anthony pulled John back into the shadows.

'It's something they don't know about—' Mr Pettigrew was saying. He had a tight, shut expression on his face.

Mr Pettigrew went upstairs.

Anthony said, 'Let's get out of here.' He moved sideways down the hall and to the front door. John followed him. Outside Anthony said, 'Bet this place is full of tunnels, attics, storerooms and secrets. I'd love to sneak back when Pettigrew is gone and search the place.'

Anthony turned away from the house. 'This is the point where we'll have to decide whether to go back or continue on.'

'I'm not going back,' John said.

They walked towards the main road. Eventually the road took them along by the seashore.

'How much further do you think it is?'

Anthony looked worried. 'I think we're lost.'

They rested on a bank, then walked again until they came to a crossroads. There was a shop and a few cottages.

'You wait here. I'll buy some food.'

Anthony bought bread and ham, a bottle of lemonade and a bag of biscuits.

'Is this the way to Gosport?' he asked the shop assistant.

'It's a long way from here, lad. About eight miles.'

They walked until their legs hurt, then rested and ate

their meal. Anthony cut the bread with his penknife and stuck the ham between two uneven slices.

When they had finished eating, they walked on. It began to grow dark and cold.

Anthony said, 'We'll have to sleep in a field, or a ditch.'

'We can't sleep outside again tonight.'

'Why not? Can you think of anything else to do? Unless you want to walk all night.'

'We could ask somebody to let us stay the night.'

'That would be a good idea if there was somebody to ask. Look around you, do you see any houses? We haven't passed one for the last few miles.'

They came to a tumbledown shed. The floor was covered with leaves and green moss. They found a dry corner to pitch the tent, then huddled down, close together. In the pitch black, John could hear rustling in the undergrowth.

The clamour of the dawn chorus woke him. It was cold and damp. A silver frost sheened the grass around the shed. They were covered in leaves, their faces dirty.

'Will we light a fire?' John asked.

'No. We'd better get going. We'll clean ourselves up when we find a stream.'

When they came to some shops, Anthony bought more bread, milk and apples. They ate in silence in a layby, near a bus stop.

At last a bus trundled up the road, and stopped beside them.

'Two halves please.'

The conductor looked doubtfully at Anthony and said, 'Oh go on then'.

Exhausted, they travelled in silence. This time the sea was on either side of the road. They arrived at Gosport. As they tramped through the streets, not knowing where to go, they felt too conspicuous to stop anyone to ask the way.

The town was strange and indifferent to their plight. People were queuing at the quayside. Anthony stopped to ask the way to the naval hospital.

'That's in Hasler,' a woman who was buying a ticket for the ferry told him. 'Not far from here, but watch out for the blue H signs. It's easy to miss the turn for it.'

They found the hospital in a remote part of the town: a magnificent red-bricked building surrounded by high walls, the tops of which were looped with barbed wire. A policeman stood in front of a security hut.

Anthony nudged John. 'Keep him talking. I'll be back,' he whispered, as he slipped away.

'What is your name?' The policeman looked down from a great height.

'John Thornton. That's a terrific tower you've got there!'

'Yes,' the policeman said, looking over his shoulder. 'They used it as a landmark during the war, to bomb other targets. That's how it was saved. Is there somebody you want to see?'

'My father. I think he might be a patient here.'

'What identification do you have?'

'Identification?'

'Yes. Means of identity. You know. Have you anything to say who you are? We can't give out information about our patients to just anybody.'

'I have no—'

'In that case, you will have to fill in a form. Name, age, present address.' He led John into the security hut.

John sat down at a desk and laboriously began filling in the form. He wondered if Anthony had made any progress as he handed back the form.

The man glanced at it. 'Come back in a few hours.'

'Thank you, sir.' John felt disappointed as he left.

Anthony was waiting for him outside the gate. 'What kept you?'

'You told me to keep him talking.'

'You did that all right.'

'Did you see anyone?'

'Yes. I asked the porter if there was a patient here called Paul Thornton. He said there was, and asked if I was his son. I said you were outside, so he said to call back later.'

'What'll we do?'

'We'll call back and see what they say.' Anthony looked at his watch. 'Let's get something to eat. I'm starving.'

'I don't want anything to eat. I want to see my father now.' John stood rooted to the ground.

'You can't see him. They won't let you. Anyway, it mightn't be your father at all. So come on.'

John did not move.

'If you don't come on, I'll split you.'

When they returned, there was a man in a Red Cross uniform waiting for them.

'You were inquiring about one of the patients?'

'Yes.'

'Will you come this way please?'

They followed him across the grounds of the hospital and into a room where two policeman were waiting. 'What's going on?' Anthony looked from one to the other.

'We've been in touch with the boy's family. His mother is on her way here.'

'You shouldn't have done that. Now we'll never find my father,' John blurted out.

'Calm down. When your mother gets here tomorrow, everything will be explained to you. Meantime I suggest you both have a bit of a clean-up. Nurse Taylor will look after you.'

17

From the time the Red Cross phoned Karen to tell her that John and Anthony were in Gosport, she had not relaxed.

'What!' she had shouted into the phone. Bill had taken the receiver from her, and held her against his chest while he made some sense out of the conversation.

Gertie started on the baking in a fit of domestic efficiency, covering her hands with dough and protesting that people still had to be fed.

Karen moved restlessly around the house, picking up the phone to make sure it was working, checking and re-checking her appearance in the mirror. Her hair was cut in a bob and she was wearing her good blue suit. She had packed a small suitcase ready to go at a moment's notice.

'Relax,' Bill had told her, over and over again.

As she waited for Bill to bring the car round, she looked at Paul's photograph and felt panicky. All the years he had been gone. Years of searching for him, of keeping his clothes aired, of not knowing how he was being treated. How much worse for him? She knew he would not be the Paul she had once known. In what way she had no idea. She was different. The insecurity of rearing her child without a husband, with no permanence in her life, had changed her from the fun-loving girl he had known, to an indecisive woman. Routine had numbed her. Could she remember him as he had been, or was her memory clouded in fantasy? What did she know about his life for the last ten years? Worst of all, what would he think of her for having doubted his existence, and falling for his cousin Hank?

When he had first gone missing, she was sick with worry, but as the years passed her memory of him dimmed, and she had to force herself to remember his face. When there was no information about him, she was filled with doubt. How could a pilot, in command of aircraft and crew, disappear? Often she had wondered if he still cared for her, if perhaps he had found someone else. Perhaps he did not want to return to her.

'Are you all right, Karen?' Gertie called up the stairs.

'Coming!' She took a last look in the mirror.

Gertie and Gran were waiting at the hall door.

'Come on, love.' Gertie put her arm around her.

Gran said, 'I can't understand for the life of me how John found his way to the bottom of England when he was supposed to be in school.'

'Anthony was with him,' Gertie said.

'Just goes to show—' she began and stopped as Mrs Quinn came to the hall door.

Mrs Quinn's hair was dishevelled, and her eyes were red-rimmed from crying. 'I don't know what Anthony was thinking of when he took John away like that,' she said to Karen. 'Honestly, I didn't know a thing about it.'

'If he hadn't been let do what he liked, it wouldn't have happened, because he would have been missed,' Mrs Keogh said. 'I always said he'd come to a bad end.'

Mrs Quinn turned on her. 'Who are you to talk? What about your own? You don't even know where your husband is this minute, never mind one of your children.'

'Leave my husband out of this,' Mrs Keogh blazed.

'Leave is right. Isn't he always leaving?'

'That's quite enough, Mrs Quinn,' Gertie said. 'No one blames you for Anthony's actions. He shouldn't have taken John away, but he meant well.'

'Meant well my foot,' Mrs Keogh began as Bill hurried Karen to the car.

'God love her,' Gran said as she waved goodbye. 'Little does she know what's facin' her.'

'First things first,' Bill said to Karen when he had brought John and Anthony back to the hotel. 'We'll have to take them shopping for some decent clothes.'

Karen hugged John. 'Look at the state of you, and you smell!'

'Did you find Daddy? Is he here?' John jumped up and down, hardly able to wait for his mother to speak.

Karen put her arms around him. 'We think we've found Dad.'

'I want to see him.'

'You'll have to wait a bit longer, darling. Daddy is not well.'

Anthony looked sheepish.

Karen burst into tears. 'You shouldn't have run away. It was irresponsible and dangerous. Why did you do it?'

'He was safe with me,' said Anthony.

'Luckily that turned out to be the case. I'm going to run a bath for John. It's all too much for me at the moment. I'll talk to you later, Anthony.'

Bill said, 'I'll take you to your room, Anthony. You'll need a good wash and shave before you present yourselves to the outside world.'

'Thanks, Mr Doyle.' Anthony began to relax, knowing that the danger of him getting into trouble had passed.

While Bill was shopping with the boys, Karen lay on her bed. Now that she was here, she was afraid to meet Paul.

Dr Armstrong was waiting for Karen and Bill in the hospital waiting room. He came quickly to meet Karen, hand outstretched. 'I'm glad you got here.'

Karen, pale and shy, sat on a sofa by the fire. Bill sat beside her and held her hand.

'When can I see him?'

'There are some medical details to be discussed first.'

'Of course, we know his health couldn't be too good,' Bill began.

'Why did it take so long to find him?'

'Mrs Thornton, your husband is suffering from amnesia. He was living in a monastery in Antwerp when he was found by the Red Cross. The monks took care of him, and in return he looked after the gardens. Apparently he was quite happy.'

Karen sat white-lipped and silent, her eyes trained on the doctor.

'Will he recognise me?'

'We are dealing here with the breakdown of the normal mental processes. He is unconsciously rejecting any previous knowledge of his life because of his horrific experiences in the war. We are hoping that your presence will jog his memory. Amnesia is difficult to understand, Karen.'

'Surely he'll want to remember Karen?' Bill looked at his daughter.

'Did you tell him that I'm here?'

'We decided not to tell him who you are, so that the immediate shock of seeing you might jog his memory.'

'May I see him now?'

'Shortly. There's one thing I haven't told you. He hasn't spoken since the war, apart from a few unintelligible phrases.' He looked at Karen. 'If his memory of you is strong, even at a subconscious level, he could recall everything. However, I urge you not to be too hopeful.'

Bill put his arm around Karen. She shivered and said, 'He loved me.'

'I understand that, Mrs Thornton, and I'm hoping that you will do wonders for him.'

Sunlight poured through the tall windows. It fell on Paul's silver hair, showing up the web of lines around his eyes. It picked out the vein that throbbed at his temple, and the fatigue that was etched through every feature of his face. At first he did not see her.

'Paul?' She thought she had cried out, but her voice was little more than a whisper. With a quick turn of his head he saw her, walked towards her, and took her outstretched hands. A slow smile spread across his face. Suddenly his features took on that same boyish expression he had had when they had first met.

'Oh, Paul, I'm so glad to see you!' His face blurred as she went to him. Her heart turned over, then raced as her breathing quickened. With a rush she was in his arms, kissing him, knowing that the rest of their lives together would never compensate for the time they had lost. He held her.

'Paul, oh Paul—' She kissed his lips.

He moved back and gazed at her. He was thinner, older, but his arms held her as she had remembered.

'I never thought I'd see you again. That's why—' her voice faltered and she buried her face in his shoulder.

He touched her hair.

'It wasn't that I ever wanted anyone else,' she continued, as her eyes searched his face for signs of his forgiveness. 'I have changed, Paul. I'm much older . . .' She shuddered at the sadness of the fact that she was thirty-two years old instead of twenty-two. 'You're safe now. You're coming home.'

He drew in his breath, and pulled away from her. Sighing deeply, he threw up his hands. His face was white and distressed. He looked around the room with the expression of a wild animal that had been hunted down and was trapped.

She felt baffled and hurt. He watched her, his eyes becoming distant as he shrugged.

'Paul.' Her voice was a cry. 'I thought you would be glad to see me. We all thought, the doctor said—' She was pleading with him, her voice tearful.

Eventually she lifted her arms from his shoulders and dropped them by her sides. 'Have I changed so much since we met? You do remember when we met? It was at the beginning of the war and you were on your first leave of absence from training.' She stopped struggling with words, sensing his separateness.

Watching him, wanting to ease his confusion, she said, 'You have forgotten, darling. That's all. We'll find a way.' She braced herself, full of doubt.

He walked to the window and gazed out, remote and preoccupied.

'I had better go.' She picked up her bag and gloves and fiddled with them as she put them on, reluctant to leave.

'You gave me this brooch.' She held up the lapel of her coat.

He looked at it and nodded. Then his gaze shifted uneasily as he rubbed his hand across his forehead. He watched her move into the shadows. From the door she said, 'I'll call to see you again. Probably tomorrow.' Her voice was gentle. 'There's someone I want you to meet.'

He inclined his head as he continued to watch her.

She pulled her coat around her and opened the door. Slowly she went downstairs, struggling to compose herself. The hospital seemed different. Shadows lengthened as the dusk gathered.

When Dr Armstrong came in with Bill, she said, 'He does know me, but he's not the same.'

'I understand,' Dr Armstrong said. 'It's difficult.'

'Difficult? It's impossible. He looks the same, older of course. But it's all gone wrong.'

'Don't give up. It's still possible that his memory could return, perhaps slowly.'

'What shall I do?'

'For the moment, nothing. Let him get used to you, then we'll introduce your son.'

'What's the use? You can't cure him. I now know why I was never informed that he was alive. How could they find him when he couldn't find himself? I never should have come. I should have let him be. I don't know if I should see him again. For so long I've lived with his memory. Now it's shattered.'

Bill looked troubled by the new steely determination he saw in his daughter. 'Are you sure that this is what Paul wants, Karen?'

'Of course he wants to be left alone. If he didn't, he'd try to remember. He doesn't even seem to make an effort.' She turned to Dr Armstrong. 'Does he want to come back to reality?'

'Now that he's seen you, I think he will. I'll have a better idea when I examine him.'

Karen stood up. 'I'm going back to the hotel now, I'll phone you tomorrow.'

Dr Armstrong walked them to the door. John and Anthony were waiting for them in the lobby of the hotel. John ran to meet her. 'Did you see him?'

Karen reached down to him. 'Yes, darling. I saw him and yes, he is your father.' She held him so tight he could hardly breathe.

Anthony felt a lump in his throat. 'Told you it was him,' he said, a smile spreading across his face.

Suddenly he scowled. 'I bet that Mr Pettigrew recognised him from the photograph and wouldn't tell us.' He clenched his fists.

Bill grasped Anthony's shoulder. 'Yes, he did. He isn't allowed to give out information about his patients.'

'He reported us though, didn't he?'

'Naturally, he would have been worried about your safety. Listen, son, you did well.' Bill shook his hand.

'When can I see him, Mom? Bill? What's the matter?'

'He's resting this evening, darling.' Karen looked at Bill for help.

'Your father's tired. Seeing your mother came as a shock.'

'Is he sick?'

'Not exactly sick. He can't remember everything that happened to him.'

'I expect he banged his head when his plane crashed.' Anthony said.

'Yes, he probably did,' said Bill.

'He might need a lot of help to get him to remember,' Karen said to John.

'I'll help him.' John looked from one to the other. 'I am going to see him, aren't I?'

'Of course you'll see him, darling. But you'll have to wait until tomorrow.'

The next afternoon Karen took John to the hospital. When she entered Paul's room, she walked slowly, tremulously. She stood before him smiling cheerfully.

'Hello, Paul. I've brought someone to meet you.'

John stood there in a blue suit, hair combed back, shoes shining, eyes full of admiration. 'Hello Dad,' he said.

Paul looked down at him, then enquiringly at Karen.

'John,' she whispered.

'John,' he repeated.

John rushed into his arms, too excited to see the look of confusion on Paul's face.

'Darling, take it easy. Daddy's not very well.' Karen tried to pull him away, but he tightened his arms around Paul's waist and would not move.

'I told Mom you would know me.' He looked at Paul with pride. 'You do know me, don't you?'

Paul nodded his head and leaning forward to meet John's gaze he said 'yes' so softly that Karen wondered if she had imagined that she had heard the word.

It was the tenderness in Paul's eyes that made her realise that he remembered something.

John was chattering. 'You never saw me before. I wasn't born when you went missing. What happened to you? Where were you all this time? I often talked to you. Did you hear me?'

'John, take it easy,' Karen begged. 'Daddy's tired.'

John withdrew and surveyed Paul's face for some answers. Paul, pale and tense, looked helplessly at Karen.

'Don't worry,' Karen said to him. 'We have the rest of our lives to find the answers. All that matters now is that we have found each other.'

18

Anthony wrote to Biddy from London. In the letter he said he was staying in a hostel and doing a lot of training for the fight, which was to be held at the Savoy Hotel the following Saturday night.

Biddy was delighted with the letter and showed it to her mother.

'You'll be getting rid of him before long,' her mother said disparagingly.

'That's a cruel thing to say. Anthony's good. He's kind. He carries home the messages for his mother.'

'He has the reputation of a hellraiser. He'll break your heart.'

'Don't exaggerate,' Biddy said, flouncing out of the kitchen.

Anthony won the fight and stayed on in London to continue his training. He wrote to Biddy explaining that he had been given an opportunity of a lifetime to train with a top London coach. He promised to write often. Biddy replied wishing him good luck, and telling him that she would save up to go over for a visit. He did not reply, and when several months went by and she had not heard from him, she thought of her life as useless. She continued to work part-time at the Roman Café, went to bed late, got up in the morning, washed her hair, played records, and ate her food. But no matter what she did, she did not seem able to convince herself that she was doing anything worthwhile.

Her anger boiled over when her mother told her repeatedly that she was wasting her time with Anthony. She realised that her feeling of uselessness was imperceptibly bound up with him.

Since Anthony had gone away, her life seemed to be going nowhere. She felt emotionally removed from everyone. Her skin was greasy and she had spots from eating too many chips. Was she was letting herself go?

'You're only looking for sympathy,' her mother said. 'Trying to draw attention to yourself. I don't know what you hope to gain from it.'

'Who asked you for your opinion anyway?' Biddy shouted, and left, banging the front door behind her.

Biddy had to be home by ten o'clock, unless she was working late. Her mother did not object to her being out late if she was earning money. Sometimes she went to the cinema with Patsy and Annie. They munched popcorn, puffed cigarettes, and blew smoke rings towards the back seats, pretending to ignore the squirming, writhing couples. Seeing them made her miss Anthony even more. Anthony had become a part of her life. He had taught her how to shoot an arrow with a bow, to catch jellyfish in a bucket without getting stung, to fish, to swim, to kiss.

Eventually he wrote to her explaining that with the boxing he had found a new freedom. 'Freedom to feel, to be somebody, to whistle or sing, to walk along the street with my head in the air, to go to work, to take time off, to fight or not to fight,' he said in the letter. A feeling of desolation swept over her as she read and re-read it. She began to think that he was lost to her forever.

It was a warm summer's day and Gran was making a lace tablecloth for Lizzie's bottom drawer. She spread it across the back of the sofa.

'It's almost finished,' she said, running her hand along the fine raised stiches.

'It's magnificent,' Gertie said. 'She'll love it.'

'It's the least I could do for Lizzie. I wove me love and prayers through every stitch. God bless them both, and may they have a happy life together. When is the weddin'?'

Gertie looked into the distance. 'I don't know yet. I was hoping she'd meet a nice doctor in England. But no, Pete Scanlon was the only one for her.'

'He's the right one for her too, Gertie. I always said it.'

Gertie sighed. 'I hope you're right.'

'Of course I'm right.' She sat down suddenly in her chair. Her face had gone pale, her eyes were half-closed. Gertie was beside her, leaning over her.

'Have you got a pain?'

Gran shook her head and said, 'I feel dizzy. It'll pass.'

Gertie ran for a glass of water and Gran was soon herself again. Not satisfied with her assurance that she was well, Gertie said to Bill that evening, 'I don't like the colour of her'.

Bill advised her to get the doctor, to be on the safe side. The doctor came and examined her. He gave her an injection and told Gertie he thought she'd had a slight stroke, and that he would send her into hospital for a chest X-ray.

'I don't need an X-ray. There's nothin' wrong with me that a pinch of bicarbonate of soda won't cure. I've lived me life. If the Lord sees fit to take me, I'm ready to go,' Gran said.

'Don't talk like that.' Gertie was shocked at the resignation in her voice.

Despite her objections, she went into Saint Michael's Hospital for tests. In the little steel-framed bed she tossed and turned and asked to go home. She talked about the wonderful doctors and nurses, and how their kindness was wasted on her when there were people who were really sick. Even when the pain in her chest got worse, she was not downhearted.

After a week she was allowed home. Some days she was well enough to sit up in bed. Other days she lay still, hardly breathing. Mrs Keogh helped take care of her, patiently feeding her slowly with a spoon. 'Come on

259

now, Mrs Doyle, you'll want to be well for Karen and Paul's homecoming.'

As soon as Lizzie returned from America, Gertie phoned her.

'I don't want to alarm you,' she said. 'But Gran is very weak.'

'I'll come home,' Lizzie said without hesitation. 'I'm dying to see you all anyway.'

Paul was transferred to a rehabilitation centre, and when Karen was satisfied that he was comfortable, she returned with a reluctant John, who protested wildly about returning to boarding school.

Sissy arrived when everyone had given up hope of her being in time. 'It was nearly impossible to get away,' she said. 'My work with the homeless takes up all my time. Anyway, Mother is a great age. I'm amazed she didn't die long ago.'

'It's no thanks to you that she didn't,' Gertie snapped, too busy with Gran to be outraged.

Gran spoke little, and slept for long stretches. She was often disoriented when she woke up.

'She's not improving,' Gertie said anxiously to Bill.

'She has a will of iron. Won't go until she decides to.'

Lizzie sat with Gran, and refused to leave her. She had every hope that she would recover. Gran was not afraid of death. Gradually she became more frail. When Karen held her hand and asked her how she was, she said that she was comfortable.

Early one evening her breathing became strangled. Gertie phoned the doctor and the priest. After her injection she fell asleep. Father O'Brien anointed her. She opened her eyes and looked all around the room and at everyone in it.

'Where's Lizzie?' she asked finally.

Lizzie reached out and took her hand in hers. 'I'm here, Gran.'

'Did they find Paul?'

'Yes, Gran.'

'Where's Vicky?'

'She'll be here soon.'

'What about Hank?'

'He's coming back to see Karen.'

Gran sighed, 'Ah what about him,' she muttered. 'My prayers were heard. John has a father. The Lord works in mysterious ways.' She spoke with great effort, then closed her eyes.

There was a stillness in the room. Gertie began to say one of Gran's favourite prayers, The Magnificat:

> *My soul magnifies the Lord, and my spirit*
> *rejoices in God my Saviour, for he has*
> *regarded the low estate of his handmaiden.*
> *For behold, henceforth all generations will*
> *call me blessed:*

For he who is mighty has done great things
for me, and holy is his Name.

Father O'Brien and the rest of the family joined in.

Gran did not speak. She lay there, a shrunken old woman with dull eyes. It was hard to recognise the Gran who had once been full of vitality, the Gran full of wisdom and love. A perceptive woman, who loved unconditionally, and had the wisdom to understand them all when they did not understand themselves. As the prayer ended, a look of recognition came over her face, and it softened into a smile. She looked around the room, at everyone in it, then turned her head towards Lizzie and was gone.

Everything went still. Her body was lifeless, and a feeling of emptiness pervaded the room. Lizzie was crying softly. She felt Gran's absence immediately and there was so much sadness in her that she was afraid she would burst.

At last Gran was at peace, the strain removed. The creases left her face, her mouth was straight. Her serene expression indicated to Lizzie that she had gone to heaven and was not disappointed.

After her body had been removed, the house felt empty, every room in it holding onto a memory of her. Her voice and her sayings were everywhere, even in the crevices of the walls. 'I speak as I find,' 'Earn gold and wear it,' 'One swallow doesn't make a summer,' 'Cut your coat according to your cloth.'

She wanted to be buried with her parents in Limerick. 'Give me a simple funeral,' she had said. They took her there, arriving late and staying overnight. Uncle Mike, Bill's brother, arranged everything. Aunt Peggy cooked a big meal for them all, and talked incessantly about Gran and the wonderful woman she was.

There was no comfort in Aunt Peggy's dulcet tones, or the food she cooked for them. The sadness was everywhere; outside in the garden, among the trees, in the birdsong that she had loved, and among her favourite flowers.

At the funeral they sang '*Nearer My God to Thee*' and '*Abide with Me*', her favourite hymn. She was often teased about it being a Protestant hymn. 'I don't care,' she would say, 'the Protestants have good taste.'

It was raining. Large heavy drops that splashed onto the coffin as it was lowered into the ground, and soaked through Lizzie's raincoat. She did not care. Her body felt empty and cold.

Uncle Mike's face was jovial but the hand he held in Lizzie's shook, and his eyes were glassy.

' 'Tis a sad day for the Doyle family,' one of the neighbours said. 'She'll be a terrible loss.'

'Oh, a powerful woman,' said another.

The priest sprinkled earth over the coffin and said, 'May she rest in peace.'

'May she rest in peace,' Mrs Keogh reinterated. 'Though I don't see how she can with all the carry on. Her curiosity will get the better of her.'

Bill moved away, not wanting anyone to see the tears running down his cheeks.

'A saint if ever there was one,' Mrs Keogh continued to Karen. 'What are you going to do about Hank?'

Karen shivered. 'He's on his way here.'

'Just think, you could have ended up with two husbands.'

'Don't remind me.'

'A lovely funeral. Beautiful mass,' Auntie Peggy said to Gertie, as they linked arms to leave the graveyard.

'She hated funerals,' Gertie said.

'Couldn't escape this one,' Sissy chimed in. 'I'm going back to the car.'

Lizzie was thinking of Gran's body buried in the chill earth, and how she did not want to leave her there. Picking her way through the tombstones, she found it physically difficult to walk. She kept her head down and did not once look back.

Later in the sitting-room Karen put her arms around Lizzie. 'Have you fixed a date for the wedding, love?' she asked.

Lizzie shrugged. 'Pete would like to have the wedding in New York. He has no family worth coming all the way home for. Now that Gran's gone, I don't see the point either.'

Karen hugged her. 'Don't make a decision yet. Not while you're upset.' She looked reflective. 'Still, wouldn't it be a lovely trip for Mam and Dad. Who knows, I might even make it, if Paul is well . . .'

The rest of the family were gathered in the kitchen. Gertie said to Uncle Mike, 'I'll never forget the time she got lost at Nelson's Pillar. Went off for a drink, if you don't mind, just as we were about to get the bus home.'

'She was a stubborn woman. Must have scalded the heart outa you betimes.'

'Oh indeed she had her moments. But she was a great woman all the same. Full of character. Afraid of no one. A strength to us all.' Her voice broke and she buried her face in her hands and sobbed.

Sissy went and put her arms around her. 'There, there,' she soothed. 'You gave her a good home, Gertie. How you put up with her I'll never know.'

'The whole of Dun Laoghaire was packed into the church the other evening,' Bill said with quiet pride.

'I didn't think they'd remember her,' said Mrs Keogh. 'She hadn't been down town for a while.'

'I dread the house without her,' Gertie sniffed.

'You'll be busy with Karen and Paul,' Bill reminded her. 'I was thinking,' he continued, 'that they could have the basement, now that the Quinns have moved out.'

'That's a good idea. Karen will have her hands full,' Gertie said.

'She'll manage.' Bill looked confident.

'How are the Quinns getting on?' Mrs Keogh asked Gertie.

'Great. Poor old Betty doesn't know herself with all the rooms. She calls down to leave Patsy in to play with John. She's come on no end since they moved. She's a beautiful girl, tall and elegant.'

'Life goes on,' Mrs Keogh said and went to answer the knock on the front door. 'Glory be to God, it's Hank!' she called out.

Hank ignored her and went straight to Bill. 'I'm sorry for your trouble, sir.' He extended his hand. 'Where's Karen?'

'Putting John to bed. They're staying with neighbours in the next farmhouse. I'll take you there.'

'I'll find it myself. I want to speak to her alone.'

'Suit yourself,' Bill said stiffly. 'It's the first turn on the left. Big grey house. You can't miss it.'

'Thanks.' Hank turned to leave.

Bill followed him out to the door. 'Karen has been under a lot of strain lately. Take it easy with her.'

'Yes sir.'

'And they lived happily ever after.' Karen put down the book she was reading to John.

'We'll live happily ever after now that we've

found Dad,' John said in a sleepy voice.

'Yes, darling, we will. Now go to sleep. I'll leave the light on for a little while.'

Mrs Creely, the owner of the farmhouse, tapped on the bedroom door. 'There's someone downstairs to see you,' she whispered to Karen.

Hank was pacing up and down the hall.

'Karen.' He came to meet her.

'Shhh.' She put her finger to her lips and led the way to the sitting-room.

'I didn't expect you to come all the way down here.'

'I've come to bring you home.'

'That's kind of you, but unnecessary. Dad bought me a car.'

'I see. You didn't mention that in your letter. In fact you didn't mention a lot of things.'

'I'm sorry, Hank. Everything happened so fast. And then Gran . . .'

'So fast that you couldn't be bothered to phone and tell me how you got on with Paul? Did it not occur to you that I'd be concerned?'

'I said I'm sorry.'

Hank sat down. 'How was Paul?'

A smile spread over Karen's face. 'Wonderful. He's hardly changed at all. Older of course—'

'I thought he'd lost his memory.'

'Yes. The doctors are hoping for—' Karen swung round

suddenly and faced Hank. 'How did you know about Paul's memory loss?'

Hank looked confused. 'You told me.'

'No, I didn't. I haven't been in touch with you since I saw him.'

Hank rose from the chair and began pacing the room. 'Must have been Gertie, or Bill. Yes, it was Bill who told me. What does it matter anyway? I need a drink. Got any Scotch in this godforsaken place?'

'Dad wasn't talking to you either because he was in England with me.'

'What does it matter?'

'I want to know.'

'Oh, all right. The International Red Cross contacted me about a year ago.' He stopped.

'You?'

'Paul had my name down as his next of kin. Well, we were reared as brothers after my parents were killed.'

'Go on.'

'They had found someone who fitted Paul's description, but he was suffering from a complete loss of memory, and couldn't talk.'

'Why wasn't I told about this?'

'I decided not to pursue it.' Hank lit a cigarette and inhaled deeply. Karen waited. 'The chances of it being Paul were so remote. And the guy obviously hadn't a clue who he was. You wouldn't want to be saddled with someone who didn't know you, or anything about his past—'

268

'Hank. You're talking about Paul, your cousin.'

Hank ignored her outburst. 'I decided not to bother you with it. You'd been through enough pain, and this could only cause more.'

'That was for me to decide.'

'Anyway, now that you have established that it is Paul, you'll have no problem getting an annulment.' His face brightened. 'We can get married immediately after that.'

'What?' Karen's temper flared. 'Are you seriously asking me to forget about Paul and marry you?'

'Sure I am. You don't know the guy any more, and he certainly doesn't know you. You're hardly going to try and pick up the threads of your life with someone who is so severely damaged. And what about us?'

'What about us?'

'You're not going to leave me for that dummy?' Suddenly Hank's face was contorted with temper.

'How dare you call Paul a dummy! He's going to get better, and I'm bringing him home as soon as he's fit to travel.'

Hank sneered. 'And where is *home* may I ask?'

'Ireland, where he belongs. He's not wanted in America.'

'You haven't thought this through. I've looked after you, Karen. Given you a home, everything you needed. Supported John.'

'You never had the time to marry me though.'

'There wasn't any great hurry, and I was trying to establish my business, you know that.'

'And desperate to get rid of John.' Karen gave him a bitter look.

Hank ignored her and continued. 'Paul isn't fit to work. What about medical expenses? There's no help in this country for invalids and orphans, never mind war heroes.'

'We'll manage. I'll get a job.'

'Doing what?'

'You seem to forget that I'm a qualified nurse.'

'You haven't worked in years.'

'With my training, any hospital will be glad of me. Especially with TB on the rise.'

Hank ground his cigarette into the ashtray. 'What about me? What about us?'

'You suited yourself coming and going to the States. Sending John to boarding school against his wishes, and mine. You bullied him, and me for that matter.'

'I don't seem to remember any complaints from you.'

'That was my mistake. I should have told you that I was unhappy.'

He went to her and tried to take her in his arms. 'You need me, honey. You can't manage without me.' His voice was soft, persuasive.

'Wrong.' Karen moved away. 'Paul needs me. You only wanted me because I was Paul's wife. You wanted everything Paul had. For a while it seemed as if you'd got it.'

'You're talking rubbish.'

'You took over the farm, the house, his parents, and his wife. No wonder you didn't want him to turn up. You had everything that rightfully belonged to him.'

'His parents depended on me. I was all they had left. I'm not hanging around to listen to this. I'll talk to you when you're in a better frame of mind.'

'Where are you staying?'

'I'll find a hotel in the city. We'll talk tomorrow.'

'I've made my decision, Hank. Paul and I are moving into the basement, and we're going to try and make a life for John. I'll send him back to the Christian Brothers. I'm sorry, Hank.'

'Sorry. Is that all you can say?'

'Yes.'

'You're the one who'll be sorry when you're stuck with an invalid in a basement. You'll regret this.'

'I don't think so.'

Hank wasn't listening. He was walking out of the door. 'Don't think you can come running back to me when it all goes wrong. Because you can't. I won't have it.'

John came downstairs as the front door slammed shut. He threw his arms around Karen. 'I'm glad he's gone. I'll help you take care of Dad.'

Mrs Creely came into the hall. 'I've put the kettle on for a nice cup of tea. Come and warm yourselves in the kitchen.'

Later, in her bedroom, Karen stood before the open window enjoying the damp air on her face, and the scent of pine from the trees. She thought of Paul. All she had from their past was a slim bundle of letters and diaries. Her memories of their early years together had become distant. She closed her eyes to recall him. His smile, his quiet voice, his eyes guarded as he watched her.

As her bare feet touched the cold linoleum, she shivered. She closed the window and got into bed. Lying there, she remembered the long evenings she had spent dreaming about Paul, when he had first gone missing. Fragments of dreams, unrelated to the stranger who was now in the rehabilitation centre in England. Was Hank right, was she taking on too much? She thought of the basement, with its dark wallpaper and cement floors. And John, his voice high-pitched with excitement as he described his father to Patsy. She had neglected John and now she owed it to him to try and make a normal life for him.

As she drifted off to sleep, she resolved to do her best. Only time would tell if she would succeed.

THE DAISY CHAIN *trilogy*

Part One

DAISY CHAIN WAR

By Joan O'Neill

Vicky asked to sit beside May Tully at school, with the excuse of getting help with her Irish. They walked home together ahead of me, sniggering at the boys. I hated them, and wished the war was over so that Vicky would go home. No such luck.

It is 1941, Britain is in the grip of the Second World War, and in Ireland, ten-year-old Lizzie Doyle is getting on with her life, trying to adjust to the 'Emergency' all around her, and the arrival of her wild cousin Vicky, from England. Vicky is trouble. She's a flirt, she's devious and she's headstrong. Can she and good-natured Lizzie ever be real friends?

'One of my all-time favourite teenage books.'
Robert Dunbar, *The Irish Times*

THE DAISY CHAIN *trilogy*

Part Three

DAISY CHAIN DREAM

By Joan O'Neill

Lizzie hardly recognised herself or her reflection in the long mirror. The bodice and waist fitted snugly, and the full skirt shifted as she moved . . . It was goodbye to carefree days, dances with the girls, trips to the cinema on a whim . . . Marriage represented responsibilities, a home of her own, children . . .

The third volume in this trilogy sees love blossom for Lizzie Doyle – as she prepares to marry her childhood sweetheart, Pete. While for young Biddy Plunkett, a chance encounter with old flame, Anthony Quinn, changes her life for ever. And though John's long-lost father, Paul, is finally home with his wife and son, a new threat to the family's happiness lurks in the wings . . .

ORDER FORM

0 340 85466 9 DAISY CHAIN WAR £5.99 ❑
0 340 85468 5 DAISY CHAIN DREAM £5.99 ❑

All Hodder Children's books are available at your local bookshop, or can be ordered direct from the publisher. Just tick the titles you would like and complete the details below. Prices and availability are subject to change without prior notice.

Please enclose a cheque or postal order made payable to *Bookpoint Ltd*, and send to: Hodder Children's Books, 39 Milton Park, Abingdon, OXON OX14 4TD, UK.
Email Address: orders@bookpoint.co.uk

If you would prefer to pay by credit card, our call centre team would be delighted to take your order by telephone. Our direct line *01235 400414* (lines open 9.00 am–6.00 pm Monday to Saturday, 24 hour message answering service). Alternatively you can send a fax on *01235 500454*.

TITLE		FIRST NAME		SURNAME	
ADDRESS					
DAYTIME TEL:			POST CODE		

If you would prefer to pay by credit card, please complete:
Please debit my Visa/Access/Diner's Card/American Express (delete as applicable) card no:

Signature .... Expiry Date: ....

If you would NOT like to receive further information on our products please tick the box. ❑